Accidents of Nature

Accidents of Nature

Harriet McBryde Johnson

HENRY HOLT AND COMPANY

NEW YORK

Henry Holt and Company, LLC
Publishers since 1866
175 Fifth Avenue
New York, New York 10010
www.henryholtchildrensbooks.com

Henry Holt® is a registered trademark of Henry Holt and Company, LLC.
Text copyright © 2006 by Harriet McBryde Johnson
All rights reserved.
Distributed in Canada by H. B. Fenn and Company Ltd.

Library of Congress Cataloging-in-Publication Data
Johnson, Harriet McBryde.
Accidents of nature / Harriet McBryde Johnson.
p.   cm.
Summary: Having always prided herself on blending in with "normal" people
despite her cerebral palsy, seventeen-year-old Jean begins to question her role
in the world while attending a summer camp for children with disabilities.
ISBN-13: 978-0-8050-7634-9
ISBN-10: 0-8050-7634-4
[1. People with disabilities—Fiction.   2. Camps—Fiction.   3. Cerebral palsy—Fiction.
4. North Carolina—History—20th century—Fiction.]   I. Title.
PZ7.J631942Acc   2005   [Fic]—dc22   2005024598

Permission for the following music lyrics is gratefully acknowledged:
"Impossible Dream" © 1965 Joe Darion and Mitch Leigh,
quoted by permission of Helena Music and Andrew Scott Music.

First edition—2006 / Designed by Laurent Linn
Printed in the United States of America on acid-free paper. ∞

1   3   5   7   9   10   8   6   4   2

*For Norma
and all my friends,
then and now*

Prologue

In the middle of North Carolina, there is a beach that has no ocean. Eons ago, the land faced the sea and the actions of surf and wind built up huge dunes. Then the waves withdrew, foot by foot, behind silt the rivers laid down. Today a coastal plain over a hundred miles wide separates the sand hills from the ocean that made them.

Now the soft rolling land is overlaid with golf courses and planned communities. Before the real estate boom, it was thought best suited to timber. Camp Courage was built on a forty-five-acre tract that had been planted in pine forty years before. Once planted, the trees were left alone by absentee owners.

With active management, the trees would have been thinned at regular intervals. The weaker ones would have been taken. The others, judged more likely to thrive, would have been nourished. The result would have been a regiment of uniform, straight trunks, ideally suited for the market, with just enough space between them to bring in machines when it came time to turn them into logs.

With neglect, however, the pines grew dense. Roots plunged deep to find the water that filtered through the sand. Trunks twisted toward the sun; limbs became so entangled that it would be hard to say where one tree ended and another began. Low to the ground grew a struggling crowd of seedlings, waiting for their chance to take over when wind or disease took down the big trees. Some made it. Young pines shot up amid the old growth.

In the deep shade below the lowest branches grew a hardy crop of weeds: nameless grasses, leaves, and vines not planted by design but accidentally sown by wind and animals. The weeds could do without sun. Their short roots found nourishment enough in the musty layer of decaying plant matter. They got their living from their own remains.

Most of the tract was covered with those woods. A single dirt road cut through the trees and brush and wound up and down and around the dunes. Not counting the lake, Camp Courage occupied about three acres. There the underbrush had been cleared away and the pines thinned. The remaining trees had room to thrive. Periodically, they were inspected, trimmed, fertilized, and protected from parasites. However, at this stage no amount of management could change their basic nature. Thin and thick, twisted and shapely, bent and straight, they remained. Unrehabilitated.

They were products of what is called the natural law of survival of the fittest. But their fitness was not defined by human needs, or market forces, or any grand design. In truth, they did not survive because they were fit. Rather, they were proven fit because they survived. They survived by accident.

Day 0

An arrival necessarily implies a departure from the place previously occupied.

My shoulders are sticky with my father's sweat where I took his arm to get out of the station wagon. We're met by a tall brunette in Bermuda shorts. "I'm Sue, the senior counselor in Jean's cabin. Carole's around here somewhere."

"Pleased to meet you." My parents speak in unison so perfect that someone really ought in some manner to express amusement. But instead Sue and Dad shake hands and my mother accepts a clipboard loaded with forms, while I sit, silent, beside the car. The sun beats down on my head.

"Has Jean ever spent a night away from home?"

My dad says, "No."

"Well," Mom adds, "only with us with her, on family trips and whatnot." She's working on the forms on the hood of our station wagon. Inside my sister Cindy is sprawled across the backseat.

Sue says, "We have a lot of first-time campers this time. Jean'll fit right in."

Mom's smile is a little rigid. "Well, I know she will. She always does. You know, she's in public high school. Going to graduate next year."

"With honors, I might add. Beta Club. Key Club. I-Don't-Know-What-All Club. And perfect attendance for seven years in a row—" Dad's habitual grin goes up a wide notch.

"At any rate," Mom says, "we thought it would be good for her to have an experience away from home. Away from us too. She needs to find out she can survive without us. She's never let cerebral palsy hold her back."

I shrug. I feel no need to prove anything, but if this is what my parents want, I can indulge them. While I'm at camp, my family will be sleeping in a tent on the beach.

"I know she'll have a great time. You're not nervous, are you?"

It takes me by surprise, her turning from my parents to me without warning, and I'm not ready to talk. I'm struggling to get words out, and I realize I don't even know what words I'm going for. There's no way out when it gets like this.

Sue jumps back in. "Hey, that's a really cute outfit." It's a culotte suit in a funny print—the words NO NO NO NO NO repeated all over.

Dad's still grinning, and I know what's coming. "Like I told her this morning: Just look at those clothes to remember what to tell the boys at camp!" He rubs my head the same way he rubbed it this morning when he made the same joke, the same way he always rubs his best dog. He always makes dumb jokes, and I always laugh. I laugh now, but I hope the talking will end soon and they'll get me out of the sun.

My mother hands Sue the clipboard. "Did I do everything right?"

Sue shows them where to sign. They sign. Along with the intake forms, I'm handed over in the sandy parking area. Mom bends down. I tilt my head up for a kiss that smells like face powder and feels like lipstick. Dad gives me a noisy smack on the forehead and a friendly slap on the back. "Now try to behave yourself, girl. Do us proud."

I wonder if it will be this hot the whole time.

That's it. I should have a spaz attack, but I don't. There should be a strong emotion of some kind, but there isn't. Ever since that August in 1970, I've pressed hard to squeeze something out of my memory, but I always find it dry. I have to accept it. When I lean back to receive good-bye kisses from my mother and father, all I feel is hot.

The doors *thunk* shut and the engine rumbles. Dad waves through the window and honks good-bye. I can't see, but I know Cindy is lolling around and Mom is worrying. Mom does so much worrying that I never have to worry about anything.

Sue lays the clipboard on my lap. "Jean, I'm going to take you to the lodge now." She pushes me toward a low building framed in natural timbers with a steep pitched roof.

"Since this is your first time at camp, I know you're wondering what it's like, and I can tell you you'll have a great time. You'll make all kinds of friends. There's a lot to do." Her voice fills the space behind and above my head. Below, my casters scrape through sand that's too loose for traction.

"I think Carole's down at the cabin. She's the other counselor. I'm sorry your folks didn't get to meet her." She doesn't give me time to talk. Maybe she thinks I can't.

"Almost everyone's here now. We have eight girls in the cabin—a full house—and we'll mix with other cabins for activities. . . ."

The one-sided conversation doesn't bother me. She means well. We get past the sand and roll onto the pavement in front of the lodge. In the heat I can smell the blacktop.

Dolly and I have been properly introduced, and she's sitting right beside me at the end of this long metal table, but clearly there's no point in trying to have a conversation with her. She's talking CP talk. I can't understand at all.

So I sit here and watch my eyes get adjusted to the inside darkness. In deep shade under the eaves, with open screens all around, you'd expect it to be cool here, but instead it's just a different kind of heat. Outside, the heat was hammered into my head; here it oozes into me from all sides. At the other end of the table I see another girl, sitting stiff and tense on the edge of a metal folding chair.

Dolly keeps on talking. She doesn't seem to care whether I understand or not. A geyser of meaningless vocalization shoots from a contorted throat toward the beams overhead. I'm not really trying, but I start catching phrases. "*The Tonight Show* . . . Johnny Carson . . . at the earliest . . . you know what I mean . . . never before midnight . . . to bed with the chickens . . . hate to complain . . . my novella . . . PRETTY RISQUÉ. . . ." Saliva bubbles up, and her right arm shoots out with force that startles me.

"I work on it constantly . . . well, you know . . . pretty steamy in spots. . . ." Her body has slipped down, almost off the chair seat; it fights against straps that are supposed to bind her waist but instead mash into the flesh under her arms. The right knee punches into her rib cage, and the left foot is pinched between the aluminum footrests of the wheelchair. It looks painful. "But here lights out at ten P.M. . . . *Tonight Show* . . . Doc Severinsen. . . ." Tangled shorts and tank top barely cover the essentials. She should wear a bib to catch all the drool.

I try not to listen, try not to look. That rigid girl at the far end of the table is tapping one eyebrow with the tips of two fingers. Her thin face is pasty white, and her hair, as short as a boy's.

"Pretty explicit. . . ."

I see a plump young woman on a stretcher, lying on her stomach, propped up on her elbows like a sunbather. She is talking to a blind girl, who gently sways from side to side.

"It takes up a lot of my time . . . novella . . . risqué in places . . . for adult readers . . . MOST definitely. . . ."

A quadriplegic is driving his electric wheelchair with his mouth. Whirring and clicking.

"Not at all what I'm used to . . . Taps . . . And I can't seem to fall asleep . . . one or two in the morning . . . Johnny Carson every night. . . ."

A boy camper and a good-looking boy counselor are talking in sign language. That eyebrow tapper across the table is still at it.

Dolly's talk swirls and spirals, around to the novella, back to staying up to watch Johnny Carson. Bedtimes and sex scenes. Dolly's voice merges with other voices, other sounds. In the high rafters, big fans churn the air, folding the smells of sweat and bug spray into sweet odors sucked in from the kitchen.

I summon the positive attitude that always serves me well. I look at Dolly. She's the worst CP I've ever seen. If the counselors can take care of her, I'll be no problem at all. I'll do fine. I always do fine—better than fine. I'm the only crippled student, ever, in my school; I'm the only crippled person in my hometown. When I was four, I was a regional state poster child; of course, at age seventeen I'm no longer so adorable as to stop traffic, but I still have my blond hair and blue eyes and skin that tans just right. I look down at my lap.

NO NO NO NO NO.

"I'll be back for y'all in a minute." Sue is taking Dolly and the eyebrow tapper away, leaving me with a ten-ounce bottle of Coke and yet another girl in a wheelchair.

"I'm Sara." She acts like I should have heard of her already. "I see you've met Dolly." She rolls her eyes. Her head, which looks fairly normal, barely reaches the table-top; it seems shoulders and arms sprout right from her seat. "This is my eighth year here. How about you?"

"My first time." I speak carefully, separating each syllable. If I take my time and people pay attention, I'm not that hard to understand.

I hear a boy's voice behind me. "Hey, Sara, I just found out you're here."

Her sharp eyes crinkle with delight. "Willie. You're a sight for sore eyes. Or perhaps—more accurately—I should say an eyesore."

"You're just as sweet as you've always been."

He steps in front of me, and the sight of him hits like an explosion of ugliness. He's skin and bones; a shocking lack of flesh in general, but with big knots of flesh on random places. Misshapen shinbones bowing over high-top sneakers. Khaki shorts flopping above giant knobby knees. A camp T-shirt, hanging loose at the waist and chest, stretched tight over a hunchback. Skin and bones. How does he move?

But it's the face— I can't look at it, but yet I see lips stretched like putty over twisted teeth, fish eyes, too far apart on his head, one sticking out, one almost buried by a bulging lump of something, flesh or bone, I don't know—

The face is just too much.

My panicking eyes jump back to Sara, Sara who now represents a place of safety. But she has no thought of me. Her eyes are locked on his, glowing gladness. "Meet Jean. It's her first year. Jean, Willie's been at camp about as long as I have. He's just finished his first year of college."

His voice speaks polite words of welcome, and I wonder what I ought to say. He must be so brave, to go to college, to face everyone looking like that. People say I have courage and determination, but he—

Does he want to hear that? I don't know. It doesn't matter, I guess. I can't talk with all these shock waves still rumbling through my body.

"She's been getting an earful from Dolly," Sara says.

I manage to shrug. Maybe I can pull myself together.

"It's okay to ignore Dolly," he says. "If you don't, she'll drive you nuts."

Sara pitches her head back and tells the rafters, "I'm writing a novella!" It's exactly like Dolly, I mean, like Dolly if Dolly were coherent. "An incredibly steamy sexy lurid pornographic novella for adult readers only! Based on my own experiences very very very very late at night, after lights out, with Johnny Carson!" I try not to, but I choke. The thought of Dolly and Johnny—

"Sara, you're awful. Be on your guard, Jean. She gets the greatest joy from making people spaz out." He drags a chair to Sara's other side and leans on her armrests in a familiar kind of way. I'd say he's getting comfortable, but how could someone like him get comfortable? "So what's the plan this year?"

"What are you talking about?"

"Don't act innocent. I've been around too long. If the plan's a secret, just say so. At least tell me who you've got."

"It so happens, I do have Margie again."

"Useful. Very useful. I've got the quad."

"Well, well. Good work. The only real talent in the whole camp."

"C'mon, give me a hint. I don't see how you're going to top the pie in the face."

"I didn't do that."

Willie turns to me, but I know he's doing it for effect, for Sara. "She never does anything. She has henchmen."

"No I don't."

"Like people with IQs under forty-five. If someone leads them astray, they don't get punished. They're incompetent. Untouchable."

"Now, I'm not admitting anything, you understand, but I have heard that if you take time to prepare an Untouchable, and prepare her well, she'll accomplish the mission to perfection and will never rat on whoever put her up to—whatever it was."

I still can't get my words together. Even my thoughts are stuttering.

He touches a gnarled hand to her skinny shoulder. "I'll see you later. Time to sneak off to my cabin."

"How about handing me that stuff from the middle of the table?"

"All that?" I ask.

"Yeah."

I figure I'll try. I reach out and rake over a tangle of Magic Markers, plastic string, and wood pieces. Sara extracts a marker and a sawed-wood disk. With her teeth she uncaps the marker and then sets to work on the wood with small, precise movements.

"Camp's pretty weird. The teenage session isn't really set up for non-MR people, but I keep coming for some reason." I look around again. MR must mean mentally retarded. There are lots of them around.

She concentrates on threading string through holes

drilled in the wood. Her long dark hair is crimped in waves like it's just been unbraided. She's wearing big round glasses, a baggy dress, and sandals. Her legs aren't shaved. What? A crippled hippie? The crippled people I've seen have been at the telethon. There we all wear our Sunday best.

Not far away, a black MR girl is peering at us sideways, over her shoulder. Sara notices her just when I do. "Margie! Hey! Guess what? I got you switched to my cabin. We're going to be cabinmates again!" The girl just stares at her feet. "Listen, Margie, do me a little favor. You see that knife up there on top of the trophy case? Can you get it for me?" She points with one thin finger. "You see? Up on top."

"Should we mess with the knife?" Margie asks.

"It's okay." She speaks with considerable authority. "I'll take full responsibility. Just pick it up by the handle, the black part. Don't touch the sharp part and you won't get cut."

The MR girl makes sure no one is looking, then reaches for the knife, lays it on the table, and skitters away.

"Margie's just a little tiny bit shy—at times." She takes the knife and, with a little grunt, scrapes the string across the serrated blade. Then she cuts a second piece.

"So what do you want your name tag to look like?"

I am puzzled.

"I'll give you some options." On a scrap of paper from the pile of supplies, she writes *Jean* three times. In block capitals, then a neat capital *J* and *e-a-n* in lowercase, and then in round cursive letters, just like the smart girls who take notes for me in school. I look around; all the name tags I see are in block capitals. That's how the counselors are making them.

"I like the last one."

She sets back to work. "Do you go to school?"

I say, "Yes." Very distinctly.

"Where?"

"Near Cha-pel Hill."

"Where exactly? Butner, maybe? You'd know Dolly."

Butner! All over North Carolina people tell jokes about "going to Butner," the place for the criminally insane and mentally retarded. When I was three years old, our family doctor urged my parents to send me. "But there was no way I could send my baby off" was how my mother told it, so proud, on the telethon. "I just kept her at home. Then I wanted her to go to school. At first they said no, but then they said they'd give her a try if her daddy built a ramp. We always treated her just like a normal girl. We didn't know what else to do."

I've started stuttering again. Sara is looking at me with an inquisitive face, waiting for me to answer her question. I drop whatever got me stuttering and start over.

"I've ne-ver been to But-ner."

She busies herself with her little project. I stare at my Coke bottle, study the green glass neck, observe the cold smoke rising. I've been left with eyebrow tappers and babblers and all kinds of strange people, left to stay for ten days at this place—a place where it seems Butner is normal and Crosstown High is unusual. Can this be an outpost of Butner? A dress rehearsal? My nerves spark with silent terror. But as soon as the terror becomes conscious, I will it away. Ridiculous. I'm not the kind of person who goes to Butner.

I draw in some Coke through a plastic straw and feel it burn cold in my throat. I listen to all the sounds around me. The voices. Strange voices. That big roaring fan.

Sara holds up my name tag. Against the fresh sawed wood, the smart-girl cursive looks cheerful. She runs the string through the holes, ties a knot, and lays it on the table. Then she lowers her head and puts on her own name tag. It has Gothic letters in green ink. This wasn't among the options she offered me, but no matter. I'm no show-off.

"So what school do you go to?"

"Cross-town." She clearly doesn't understand. I spell, "C-r-o-s-s-t-o—"

"Oh, Crosstown. Crip school or Norm school?"

Puzzlement spreads across my face.

"Do you go to a crippled school or a normal school?"

"Nor-mal. It's a small town. There is no crip-pled school

there. Just one high school. I am a ris-ing sen-ior. Do you go to nor-mal school?"

"Not yet. I've been in Crip school, but at the end of this past school year, my teacher told my mother she can't teach me anymore, so I'm out. The public schools don't take Crips, so I'm going to a private school. An all-white private school, no less. You know, our crippled school has been integrated for years, maybe always. I figure they don't care enough about us to bother about segregating us. Or maybe they figure we're our very own race, like the Chosen People, except no god has ever promised us any-thing that I know of.

"I don't like the idea of a Segregation Academy, and neither do my folks. But what can I do? This private school is taking me because my mother has a friend on the fac-ulty. I guess I should be grateful. Maybe I'll like it. I don't know. They have serious teachers and a library and even a language lab. But Crip school is great because we're all crippled—it's truly bizarre—and there's only one Repub-lican in the class!"

My parents voted for Nixon in the last election and for Goldwater before that. But that's none of her business.

"Maybe you can give me some lessons on how to be a Crip in Norm school. I'll have to start figuring that out, I guess."

"I don't think of my-self as crip-pled. I'm like eve-ry-one else."

"Aw, come on. You're a Crip. Otherwise you wouldn't be in Crip Camp. Say it loud, 'I'm crippled and proud!'"

I can't argue. The James Brown imitation, so unexpected, sets me off again.

I'm still choking when the counselors come back. "Oh, good, someone made your name tags," Sue says. She picks up the knife and mutters, "Oh dear, did I leave this here?" Sara gives me a conspiratorial look. No one has to take responsibility.

Sue puts the knife back, then bends down behind me and slaps off my brakes. The other counselor, Carole, takes Sara, and side-by-side we ride past the flagpole, into the pine woods.

The camp looks like a normal camp, or what I imagine a normal camp might look like, except maybe a normal camp wouldn't have blacktop on the narrow paths that wind through the woods. The asphalt makes the ride nice and smooth. It's so quiet I think I can hear our axles ringing, two faint notes in odd harmony with each other and with the song of a distant bird. The bird goes quiet and stillness surrounds us. We roll forward. Our damp skin breaks through the wall of air that was undisturbed until we came.

Midway down, a chunk of the hill has been lopped off to make space for four cabins. We veer toward one that hangs suspended on piers over the hill's downward slope.

"Hooray! We're on stilts," Sara says. "The other cabins don't cool off even at night."

Her hard little casters rattle over the planks of the gangway. Following right behind, my wide tires roll across the boards with a calm drumbeat. Just as I catch a quick look at the sudden drop below, I feel Sue pressing my tip-bar with her foot to smooth the bump at the threshold. It's an experienced foot.

"Oh, that's awfully cute," Sara says. A homemade sign— PRIVATE! COUNSELORS ONLY! KEEP OUT!—is posted on plywood that separates one corner from the rest of the cabin. In the open space, eight army cots are lined up with eight footlockers. My bed, in fact every second bed, is made upside down, pillow at footlocker. Why?

I don't ask, but Sara answers anyway. "You know, they go berserk if we turn the pillows around; they say it's a fire regulation, like they measure crowding from head to head, but I don't buy it. They do it to keep us from talking at night."

It's a big screened room under a pitched roof, built entirely of pine. With no plaster or Sheetrock to conceal the structure, I can see how the pine has been reduced to planes and right angles, cut into boards of standard dimensions that fit together according to standard plans. With no paint to cover the surfaces, I can also see the wood's surviving essence, its fiber. Now exposed, flowing whorls and knots speak of when these boards were the flesh and blood and bones of trees that drank water and ate dirt and breathed sun to grow tall in some place very much like this place where I now find myself. I like knowing that. But I also like the linoleum floor, a perfect product of chemical engineering and factory magic, shiny and hard and the color of sand.

Most of all I like the way the cabin hangs among the tops of the trees that grow from the hill below us. Now I know what a tree house is like. Turned away from the path and the other cabins, I can pretend we're far from civilization. There are no walls, just open screens; a thick tangle of trees and vines is our only drapery. Peeking through the green lace curtain, the sun plays games with light and shade. The heat has released its grip. The two oscillating fans have fresh air to work with.

"Well," Sara says, "it looks like we've got about the right mix—three wheelchairs, a one-leg amputee, two MRs, and two walkie-talkies."

"What?"

"Walkie-talkies. Campers who can walk and talk and look like Norms. Diabetics, epileptics, crazies, whatever. Some of them are more messed up than we are. Eventually it always becomes clear. They want to belong, you know."

The luggage has been brought down and is being unpacked. I grab my suitcase and throw it onto my cot.

"Not bad, Spazzo," Sara says. From across the room,

Sue gives her a stern look, but I'm not offended. She winks and keeps on talking.

"The counselors this year seem back to normal. Therapeutic recreation types. You know, in '68, we were taken over by hippies, with just a few College Republicans, enough to keep the hippies stirred up. It was a trip. On talent night we did protest songs. It was great. Then, last year, it was Jesus Freaks. They were wilder than the hippies. One of my counselors was exactly like that joke that was going around: 'I used to be messed up on drugs and sex, but now I'm messed up on the Lord.'"

I give a little snort. The joke is new to me. I work my fist around the suitcase buckles, whack them hard, and the suitcase pops open. Then, with a jerk of my sneaker foot, I flip the lid of the footlocker. Inserting fingers into a hole, I hoist up the tray and chuck it onto the bed. One by one, I slam shampoo, soap, hairbrush, and deodorant onto the tray. Hooking the strap of my camera case on my thumb, I swing it, gracefully I think, onto the ledge under the screens. A scrapbook comes next. Then I dump a UNC teddy bear on my pillow. Next I start on the clothes, but all I do is scramble them.

"Margie did a really nice job when she unpacked her stuff," Sara says, nodding toward the black MR girl. "I think she could get your clothes straight for you."

Margie looks at my clothes with the corners of her eyes, her close-cropped head bent toward her feet.

"Have you met our new Fearless Leader? I mean Camp Director," Sara asks. I shake my head no. "He looks like a pretty harmless fellow."

I'm barely listening. Sara's talking is getting a bit tiresome. Margie has crept over and is laying out my clothes on the cot, displaying their department-store newness for everyone to see. Careful brown hands smooth the bright white underwear, crisp shirts and shorts, and bouncy T-shirts and lay them in the trunk. She has a system. On the right, panties, shorts, slacks—everything for the bottom half of the body; on the left, bras, shirts—for the top half. The flowery dress befuddles her. After considerable mulling, she rolls it up. In cupped hands, she takes it up, as tenderly as she'd hold a nest of baby birds, and settles it in the gap between the two piles.

"Thank-you, Mar-gie."

I'm interested to see what's coming out of the suitcases. Sara has five baggy cotton dresses and five pairs of underpants, two nightgowns, one bar of soap, one comb, one tube of sunscreen. No extra shoes, no swimsuit, no bra, no stockings, no socks. No toys. No toothbrush. But she has a sewing kit, typing paper and envelopes, two library books, a sketch pad, and a box of artist's pastels.

"It'll probably be a little duller without the Jesus Freaks," she says. "I wonder what they're doing this summer? Are they serving the Lord somewhere else, do you think, or are they born again, as non–Jesus Freaks?"

I shrug.

"So now we're back to giving outrageously healthy, preprofessional types a little real-world experience. It's a big job, but, hey."

I consider the counselors, watch them at work. Sue. Tidy and efficient. Camp T-shirt, with crutch-and-pine-tree logo, neatly tucked into her shorts, medium-brown hair looking just-brushed in a perfect pageboy. And the other one, Carole. Petite frame overwhelmed by a baggy sweatshirt from St. Andrew's College. Red hair, about shoulder length, not quite confined by multiple barrettes and rubber bands that seem to have been added at different times during the day as the need arose. Like all the counselors I've seen, they're clean-cut but not square, in good shape but not jocks. Sara's description is accurate as far as it goes, but it makes them seem like comic-strip characters when, really, they're just normal people.

I can imagine Sue, after college, working as a physical therapist or teaching MR kids. She's competent, in control. Now, Carole seems different. She catches my gaze. "Need anything? Bathroom?"

I nod. Might as well get it over with.

Six toilets, and no stalls. I'm glad no one is here but Carole and me.

"You'll tell me what to do, okay?"

With both arms, I grab the steel handrail beside the john. I press my heels hard onto the floor, and I'm up.

"Get my pants."

She gets my culottes and underpants down in one quick tug. I release one arm from the handrail and raise one foot off the floor. I pivot on the other heel and catapult myself around the rail. I land, hard, on the toilet seat. I can't believe how loud the pee is, falling in the water. Up to now, my mother has always been around to help. Now she isn't, but it's all right. I stand up and point to the toilet paper with my chin. Carole wipes. "Okay?"

I nod, and she pulls up my culottes. In an instant, I whirl back into my chair and we're laughing together with surprised relief. A clump of red hair has escaped from the ineffectual hold of those barrettes.

All through supper and evening orientation, I heard that cot calling me. Now I sit and wait my turn for help going to bed, and I ache for the opportunity to stretch my body and hand it over to sleep. It has been a long day.

It's Sara's turn. "You ready?" Carole asks.

"Sure. Just catch me." Carole's arm is waiting when Sara flops backward. "Pull my knees up in the air, way up." Carole pulls until she's stretched most of the curve out of Sara's spine. "Great."

Sara does have a torso, after all. All day it was collapsed like an accordion. Now, she lets the air fill her bellows, in and out. Following precise instructions, Carole balls up a pillow, stuffs it under Sara's bent knees, and pulls the sheet up to her chin.

I transfer into my cot as a creaky recording of taps wails from a loudspeaker up at the lodge. Carole pulls up my sheet and thermal blanket, so slowly I could easily have told her to do something different if I wanted to. She pushes my wheelchair against the screened wall, out of the way.

Sue says, "It's lights-out. No talking."

"Unless it's a dire emergency, okay?" Carole adds.

On the last baleful note, Sue switches off the lights. I crane my neck to see the yellow bug lights go off in the other cabins. Behind me, they close the straw blinds. On the woodsy sides, they leave them up to let in the night air. It's cool now.

In the dark, I see the moon glimmer through the trees. In the silence, I hear crickets chirping. At home, we turn off the air conditioner and open the windows on nights like this. I wonder if my family can hear crickets in their tent on the beach. Do crickets live beside the ocean?

Soon the sound of crickets merges with whimpering from one of the beds. Someone is homesick; I can't tell who. Not Sara; maybe the next girl over, the MR girl, Margie. I want to ask. However, despite years of speech therapy, I am unable to whisper. There's nothing to do but sleep.

Day Two

*One defining element of consciousness is the ability
to see one's self as an object among other objects.*

My heart's pounding and I'm sitting up, too startled even
to wonder where I am. On one side, a voice whispering,
"Is someone having a seizure?" The whisper comes from
that little lump in the next cot. Sara. On the other side, a
commotion. Yes. A crash from that direction was what
woke me up.

"Who is it? Is it Denise?"

Yes, Denise. The black walkie-talkie. I glimpse pieces
of her on the other side of Sue and Carole. Sue goes for a
pillow, and I get a clear view. My heart jumps; around me
things shift into slow motion.

Carole squats on bare feet in a pool of urine and gives
all her calm, her quiet, her sober attention to the flailing
thing on the floor. It is Denise but not Denise. It's a body
in motion, motion weird and unnatural, something I've

never before seen or imagined, but also strangely like something remembered.

It's like my sister's dancing skeleton. Cindy got it one Halloween when we were small, a set of plastic bones loosely connected by ligaments of fishing line, hooked at the skull to a Popsicle stick. Cindy shook the stick, and the skeleton danced. Harder she shook it, and wilder it danced. Pinwheel arms. Piston legs. Whipping spine. A ballet of unnatural impossible movements.

Dem bones, dem bones.

But this isn't a game. This isn't a toy. These dancing bones are covered with living flesh, and the meat too is dancing, forming chorus lines of convulsions under the skin.

"Let's get her clear of the cot," Sue says, and the two counselors pull the flailing body away from the iron frame. They scrunch the pillow under the head and try to keep it there. Thousands of twitches overtake hands, arms, feet, legs, spine, neck. Some explode like volleys of machine-gun fire; others click with player-piano precision. Following their own rhythm, the actions seem deliberate, the product of a powerful force.

Is it the Devil, like in Bible Days? No. A devil would look more human. Those eyes stare but don't see; there's no spirit behind them. The force must be unconscious. Something like electrical current.

We wait I don't know how long. I want to yell "stop!"

but there's no one to yell at, nobody shaking a Popsicle stick, so I wait and wonder if her muscles will get exhausted or how it will end. I think the rhythm may be breaking. Yes, it's winding down. Stopped. Denise is asleep, snoring deep in her chest. Carole drops down to her knees. She hasn't noticed the pee, I think. Or, wait, yes, she has: She's purposefully dragging Denise out of it. She stretches Denise's long limbs, aligns her head on the pillow, and tidies the collar of the pink pajama top. Sue is up, going after the mop. It's over. The smell of Pine-Sol fills the air.

"Who was it?" Sara repeats. "Denise?"

I nod. I'm shaking.

"You've never seen that before, I bet," she says quietly. "It's pretty horrifying, no matter how often you see it. *Grand mal*. 'Big bad.' At least they've quit using tongue depressors."

We're all awake, and reveille has passed unnoticed. Sue and Carole busy themselves with other things. "Put your bathing suits on under your clothes! Swimming today!" Sue chirps.

Not one word about what's happened. As quietly as I can, I tell Sara, "It looked like she was being elec-tro-cu-ted."

"I guess she was. The brain sends electrical impulses through the nerves down to the muscles. She got too much current. You know, this place is full of electrical problems. Like you: With CP, your brain doesn't regulate the current right. With me, my brain generates fabulously well, but there's some kind of short where the signal hits the muscles. The muscles get corroded from lack of use. Maybe we all need rewiring. Hey, if we got rewired, do you think we'd be the same people?"

I shrug. All around beds are squeaking. The screen door slams behind Sue and Mary, the eyebrow tapper, as they leave for the bathroom. People are talking. Talking about things of no consequence.

"Sorry," Sara says, still flat on her back. "A little too philosophical for this hour of the morning."

As Sue dresses me, I ponder Sara's question. I stick out arms and legs to sleeves and pants, I lurch onto the toilet, and I wonder. Would I be the same person without CP? My parents always say CP doesn't matter. I am just like a normal girl. But I wonder.

We wait outside while black women put breakfast on the tables. When the call is given, we enter, cabin by cabin, filling the lodge from back to front. I'm ravenous. Watching the flow, I fall into a daze.

"It's kind of hypnotic, isn't it?" Sara makes me jump—to her obvious amusement.

"About four years ago, I was watching this completely autistic guy staring at everyone coming in to eat, like you were just now. He seemed to be looking right through them. But really he was perceiving something. The movement I guess. Because all of a sudden, without unfreezing that aussie statue-face, he says, 'Head 'em up—mooooove 'em out.' So perfect!"

True. It is like a cattle roundup. We join the slow-moving herd inside, and I am corralled with Sue on one side, Sara on the other.

At the table are ten identical plates of grits, scrambled eggs, and toast. Sue fetches three mugs of coffee—one for herself, one for Carole, and one for Sara. The rest of us get milk. Dolly addresses the ceiling, and my ears catch scattered phrases from the outpouring, "Coffee . . . I COULD SURE USE . . . get moving . . .VERY late . . . I stay up with JOHNNY."

Sara whispers, "At Butner I bet they start putting people to bed when the three P.M. shift comes on."

I raise my eyebrows at Sara's coffee, and she explains, "They don't give coffee to campers, but my doctor lets me fill out my own medical form. I write up everything I want. Under a question about constipation—positively an obsession around here—I put 'Laxatives only upon request; A.M. coffee for regular bowel function.' They never question a doctor's order."

She's talking low and fast. The lodge is so noisy that no one can hear anyone else unless they really listen. No one is listening now. Sue is close enough to hear, but she's busy feeding me and Mary and herself.

"What else is on your me-di-cal form?" I open my mouth to a forkful of eggs.

"Oh, all kinds of things. I have bed baths and use a bedpan—showers annoy me and my days of balancing on toilets are done. I must not be compelled to eat any food I don't like. My photograph may not be taken."

I make my eyebrow ask why.

"One year my face wound up in the camp brochure over the caption, 'Smiling through the tears.' That will never happen again!"

On seeing Denise now, helping with cabin cleanup, it's hard to connect her with that flailing body. She looks so normal with that shiny black plastic headband over her flip hairdo, a touch of lipstick and blush brightening skin one shade darker than a paper bag. There might be some weariness in her deep-set eyes, something suggesting a human soul who had a bad night, but in all her actions she's alert, with-it, cheerful. Playfully, she slaps Margie on the back. "She's the Queen of Clean! Come on, Your Majesty, show us how!"

Somewhere Margie has learned how to make a bed with hospital corners. The others are paying close attention.

"Hey, y'all, we've got the competitive edge!" Sara says. "Not a word to the other cabins about our hospital corners, y'all. Margie, be on your guard. My buddy Willie will be all over you looking for information."

Yvonne, the one-leg amputee, is pushing the dust mop. "Do you think we could win Cleanest Cabin?"

"Sure, no problem, if you want to. In fact, since we have Margie, it's hardly a challenge."

"Might as well go for it," Denise says. "And didn't he say—What's his name—the director?"

"Bob."

"Yeah, Mr. Bob. He said cleanup was fifty percent of Best Cabin All Around."

"Six-ty per-cent," I say. I paid attention at last night's orientation; like all good students, I know the importance of the scoring system.

"And we'll win Talent," Sara says. "Count on that. I'll write the skit. We'll give it to 'em. Ka-boom! The visitors will go ape."

"What visitors?" Denise asks.

"Oh, the Jaycees. They raised most of the money to build the camp, you know, and they always show up in force for the last session. And we may even be graced by the presence of our Major Benefactor and Pillar Extraordinaire, the Honorable State Senator B. J. McNeill.

"But remember!" Sara sniffs and cocks her head, part Mr. Bob and part Barney Fife. "Cleanup is CRITICAL! While you're in morning activities, MIS-TER Bob, our Fearless Leader, our Little Father, our Alpha and Omega, will be performing inspections. Personally! He will crawl under every single cot to look for dust. Personally! He'll climb up into the rafters to hunt cobwebs. Every cot must be made up! Every corner absolutely clean! Got it?"

"Got it!" they yell.

Margie walks from cot to cot, checking those corners. The walkie-talkies are sweeping. I spot some cobwebs and tell Sara, and Sara tells Yvonne the one-leg amputee. Mary the eyebrow tapper is tapping something with a paper towel. Dolly is the only one who isn't involved. She's busy blabbing.

Margie smooths the ghost of a wrinkle out of Yvonne's bedding. "They look so nice!"

"I'd say we're done," Sara says.

Margie walks over to me, her head turned sideways. "You want me to push you to swimming?"

I nod. I have my doubts, but I don't want to hurt her feelings.

We're over the gangway, headed down the hill. Just in time, I feel Margie's firm backward tug on my push handles. Maybe she learned to push wheelchairs wherever she learned about hospital corners.

We come to the lake in bathing suits and lay our towels on the strip of white sand at the shore. Other things too are dropped there: seven or eight wheelchairs, assorted crutches and canes, chest harnesses for hearing aids, helmets, and arms like Captain Hook's. A pair of full leg braces, joined at the top, lie with a back and neck brace.

In steel, leather, and canvas, it's the shell of an exoskeletal camper.

Here's a boy I've seen before. I took him for a walkie-talkie in the lodge yesterday. Now he sits on a towel, disconnects both legs, and drops them on the ground. At first glance, what's left of him looks like a half boy, literally truncated, a wartime fatality, you'd think. But then I watch him cross the sand on his rump and two strong arms. Free of the weight of fake legs, he speeds into the water, a place where the lackings of legless creatures are unimportant.

A boy counselor straps me into a life vest and walks me into the cold black water. With every step, I make a big splash and feel my heels push deep into the sand. My long legs don't work right, but I'm proud to have them, proud in fact of all my body parts. At the same time, I'm not disgusted by the others, people with pieces missing or mangled. I count it a rare privilege to see them all without their coverings, their equipment, their attachments, their replacement parts, as they really are, in all their strange variety.

I pass Denise. She's staying near the edge, maybe afraid of what could happen if she gets in too deep. For a moment the memory of this morning has me spooked, but I splash my way forward and realize that witnessing that force overtake her—even that horror—is part of the privilege. I've seen Denise up close, learned her secret. I've seen her as she's never seen herself.

Beyond the floating barrels the lake gets deep, but here the slope is very gradual. I go forward until the water grabs my life vest and yanks me up. My feet lose contact with the earth, and, shivering with the wonderful cold, I lie back. The boy counselor lets go. At first he stays close enough to touch me; then he lets me drift and I am off, floating on my own.

I give myself over to floating. I close my eyes to the sun. On all sides I hear voices, but I don't try to make them out. My mind clears itself of conscious thought. I do nothing. I simply am. I luxuriate in absolute passivity, the passivity of a happy infant. In my mind, I am an infant again. A happy baby.

They always said I was a happy baby, once things settled down. I've heard the story many times. The very beginning was rough. I tried to enter the world shoulder-first and barely came through the struggle of being born. My mother labored, hour after hour, until the doctor finally got me turned around. "By then," Dad always says, "I was scared to death that I'd lost them both." I came out blue. The doctor massaged me, slapped me, blew air into me. The standard routines to stimulate breathing. At first nothing. But then I responded. With a desperate gasp, I swallowed my first gulp of air. I was alive. "That doctor nearly keeled over," Dad says. "See, he wasn't expecting Little Miss Jean to make it. She surprised him, and good."

Was the surprised doctor glad or sorry? I was without

oxygen for a long time. Surely the doctor knew I was brain damaged.

For weeks, my little body trembled and twitched in an Isolette. Sucking didn't come naturally, but they fed me from a syringe and I choked down enough to live. And then, at three months, I discovered how to swallow. "Once she got the hang of it," Dad jokes, "there was no stopping her. She eats us out of house and home!"

"Now, Billy, cut that out," my mom always says. I always laugh.

By the time I started swallowing, I was nice and pink. Soon I got plump, just like a normal baby. My mother and father had come to love me.

"Baby Jean was so special," my parents say. I was immersed in their love; they treasured me all the more because my life had come so dear. Freely they gave me all I needed. And seventeen years later, they still feed me, bathe me, and dress me with the same care they gave me when I was an infant. In return, all they ask is that I be happy. It's a good bargain. I've kept my side of the deal. I float, placid, calm, absolutely content in the water's embrace. Just as I am meant to be.

Reality intrudes with the sound of Sara's voice. "Hey, Jean." The sound is close, but I can't find Sara in the water. I look up. The sun overhead almost blinds me, but I finally make her out. Up on the dock, alone, still in her dress, still in her wheelchair, drawing a picture.

"Never in my life have I seen a spazzo look so relaxed! Who'd'a thunk it? A spazzo! As relaxed as a fat, lazy, happy walrus on *Mutual of Omaha's Wild Kingdom.*"

I don't try to speak. A fat, lazy, happy walrus would not make the effort. I just float.

Within seconds after I've come out of the lake, a coating of algae has dried tight and grainy on my skin. When they ask if I want to be in the first shift in the girls' showers, I squeal enthusiasm. Now clean, still cool, I'm content to sit in the cabin and wait for the others.

Sara is sitting cross-legged on her cot. No swimming, no shower. "Looks like we have some time to kill." She closes her book. "I see you brought a photo album. Could I look at it?"

I fling the book in front of her, transfer myself onto the bottom half of her bed, and watch her turn through seventeen years of photos, which my mother has carefully labeled. Christmas mornings, birthday parties, cookouts. A one-story wood-frame house with a pecan tree in the yard, a backyard garden with tomatoes and green beans, small tidy rooms with wall-to-wall carpeting. A console TV. A smiling family—a mom and a dad and two girls. Each picture illustrates a typical small-town family of modest means. A perfectly normal family, normal except for the much-loved crippled daughter.

Margie kneels on the floor beside us and marvels as the

pages flip by. I don't know whether she finds something particularly amazing in each picture, or whether it's the idea of a scrapbook itself that has her so astonished.

Along with the photos there are newspaper clippings from the Crosstown weekly, and a few from the Chapel Hill paper. Sara reads the headlines to Margie. "Crosstown Cripple to Lead Fire Parade . . . makes Honor Roll . . . gets award . . . Poster Child." There is a telethon flyer for nearly every year of my life. An eight-by-ten version of my poster. "Gracious peace!" Sara says. "The Crosstown Cripple sure gets a lot of press! Who's your agent?" She's mocking me, but I don't mind.

She stops at a full-page story, "Crosstown Girl Learns to Walk." In the photo, I'm seven years old, adorable, with an enormous grin. I'm standing on full leg braces, my hands squeezing a walker. Sara reads it aloud, the whole story: four years of physical therapy, two operations, the high cost of keeping a growing child in braces. Proud parents. Courage and determination. "This little girl is an inspiration" is what my physical therapist said.

She looks at me with gravity. "It looks like a good part of your childhood was swallowed up with all this walking stuff." She pauses. I shrug.

"It is funny. Therapists, teachers, relatives—everyone— they all think walking is such a wonderful thing. And we don't question that. We believe it must be worthwhile, or they wouldn't torture us for it. And then, finally, you get up on your feet, take a few halting steps—pardon me, I mean courageous and determined steps—and the cameras flash, and everyone's inspired. But then you find out walking is a lousy way to move from place to place. And as you get bigger, it's worse. When you fall down, you have farther to go. When you start to think for yourself, you realize a wheelchair is a better way to get where you're going."

"The wheelchair's nice," Margie says. She plucks Sara's metal spokes. Each sounds a different tone.

"Yeah, Margie, it is nice," Sara says.

"Did you e-ver walk?" I ask Sara.

"No. I did crawl when I was very small, but my legs were so weak there was no serious effort to make me stand, thank God. But I did my time in PT. It's unavoidable. My PT couldn't do anything for me, really, so she got obsessed with the fact that my knee tendons were drawing up and my legs wouldn't straighten. She was a German woman. 'Schtraighten your lecks,' she'd say, 'or ze kontraackchure vill get vorse.' I complained about her so much that my ma started referring to her as the Bitch of Buchenwald. 'How'd you get along with the Bitch of Buchenwald today?' she'd ask. One day I asked her, 'What's Buchenwald?' She told me all about Hitler, the Jews, the camps, the ovens, and the medical experiments. It blew me away. I was only about eight years old, and I had no idea. Then I asked, 'Mama, what's a bitch?'"

I snort; it's a funny story, whether true or not. But Sara

isn't laughing. She leans forward and shifts her weight from one elbow to the other.

"You know, my mother made light of it, but all that yanking and pulling really hurt. And what's really weird is that I went through it for about two years of my life and no one asked why. The Bitch never explained why I needed to have straight legs. When they started talking about surgery to cut my tendons, the light finally dawned on my parents and I got out of PT for good. Ze kontraackchure got vorse, as predicted, but it didn't matter at all. So I sleep with pillows under my knees!"

Sara's cot creaks as I pull my feet up on the mattress. I wrap my arms around my suntanned knees, not quite concealing the thin, pale lines where my legs were cut to release drawn-up tendons.

Sara is waiting for me to say something, but I don't know what to say. My parents saved that article about me walking to celebrate a brief triumph; all these years it has remained in my scrapbook as a permanent reminder of my only real failure, a disappointment none of us wanted to talk about.

Can a wheelchair be a choice, and not a failure? I'm not sure. Maybe Sara was abused by her physical therapist; surely for most people it makes sense to try to become as normal as possible. But what if normal isn't the only way to be? It's an oddly thrilling idea, but I'm not ready to put it into words.

So I ask, "Do you have any pic-tures?"

"Just one." She opens her book and takes out a photograph she's using for a bookmark. "Here we are. Grandmother's porch on Thanksgiving."

The big house with white columns looks like something from *Gone With the Wind*. Margie gasps.

"We have the trappings of privilege because my mother is from the landed class. But not lots of cash."

In my holiday pictures, fathers wear hunting shirts and mothers, pantsuits—while children are dolled up in formal clothes. Sara's people are the opposite. Her parents are dressed up in dark suits. Sara and her sister are in hippie dresses; the three little brothers sport blue jeans and disheveled mops of long hair.

"What does your father do?" I ask.

"My parents are *both* college professors."

I ignore my little gaffe. "So that's where you get it."

"What?"

"You talk like a pro-fes-sor."

"Sorry about that." She doesn't sound at all sorry. "I do like to talk. A whole lot. It's my specialty. I know it might be hard for you to get a word in edgewise. Just hit me or something. I am trainable."

"Okay. I will. Ne-ver fear."

"It's time to play—*Let's Make a Deal!*" In the lodge after supper, a boys' counselor does a passable imitation of the game show host, Monty Hall. But I've never seen Monty

Hall take pains to explain that once you make a deal, you can't unmake it. And Monty never protects contestants from winding up with the booby prize. This guy does.

Each of us has brought something. One by one, we go forward and exchange our things for prizes that counselors have hidden in boxes and behind curtains. Some of our things wind up back on the trading floor. Someone gets Sara's camp T-shirt from 1965. Someone else winds up with my Tar Heel pennant. Like most campers, I get one trade and I'm done; occasionally, when the MC spots a good sport with entertainment potential, he lets the trading get more elaborate.

Hideous Willie starts with a well-worn paperback spy novel and completes multiple transactions. His spy novel comes back to him. He's offered another trade. He agonizes. Curtain or box?

Finally, he opens the box. "This is it, Monty! No way am I trading this away!" With a flourish he holds up his prize: a can of Spam. It's supposed to be a booby prize. "I'm starving! I was just thinking, 'How will I make it to breakfast?' Now, this is great!" In front of all of us, he opens the can and eagerly stuffs his misshapen mouth with grayish gunk. The audience groans. Willie attacks the Spam with moans of ecstasy.

"Sit down, Willie!" Monty yells.

Willie takes a chair behind Sara and me. He's still eating the Spam. I can smell it.

Sara whispers, "You're making me sick."

"I know. Someone's got to do it."

Now a counselor comes forward leading a pale man dressed completely—from canvas fishing hat to socks—in yellow. He walks on the balls of his feet in a rather dainty way. He's a full-grown man, maybe only a year or two older than the rest of us, but tall and solid, with a body of normal shape and function. But never would he be called a walkie-talkie.

"Oh, God," Sara says, "this should be wild. They say Robert is PMR—profoundly mentally retarded—but he's so aussie, who can tell?"

Before I got here, I'd never seen an autistic person, but already I can spot the signs. Robert's movements are odd, surely, but his face is odder still. It doesn't smile or frown or show any emotion. It might be called a blank stare, but it isn't at all like Denise's empty seizure-face. That was really blank. Inhuman. Robert's face is human to an extreme. It is the face of a person intensely preoccupied. If you look only at his face, you'd never guess that what he's staring at isn't really there.

"Hey, Robert! Time to play—*Let's Make a Deal!*"

His gaze remains fixed at middle distance. Even though I know there's nothing there, I find myself imagining what he might be looking at. He could be a violin player at his music stand. His whole world is a little less than three feet away and about eight inches below his eyes.

"What do you have to trade, Robert?" Monty asks.

Robert is oblivious to all the activity around him. He stands with one foot turned out and stares to his right, at his special downward angle. He could be a shopper considering an item on the grocery shelf. He sticks out his right index finger and moves it clockwise, almost completing a small circle. Then he returns to the starting point and makes that circle, over and over again.

"Robert, do you have something?"

Robert makes those dainty little circles. Monty looks down at Robert's left hand. "Aha! A package of Juicy Fruit gum. Stretch your coffee break, huh? Well, if you'll give it up, I will offer you what's in the box or what's behind the curtain."

"Take what's behind the curtain," a guy in the audience yells.

"Behind the curtain, behind the curtain, behind the curtain, behind the curtain," Robert repeats in a hollow voice.

"THE BOX!" another boy yells.

"Theboxtheboxthebox," Robert mutters.

"Does he know what he's say-ing?" I ask Sara over all the racket.

"I imagine not."

People shout out advice, and Robert repeats whatever sounds register in his brain.

The legless boy yells, "GOLDSBORO!"

"Gotta Goto Gozeboro, Baby, Heh-Heh-Heh, Gotta Goto

Gozeboro," Robert repeats, this time in bell-clear tones. Then he smiles, as though remembering some secret joke.

I raise my eyebrows at Sara. "That's his mantra," she explains. "He's been saying that for years. Nobody knows what the deal is. He lives at Butner, and nobody knows of any Goldsboro connection. It might have something to do with Cherry Hospital. Or he might just like the sound. But once he starts saying it, well, we could be here all night."

The exasperated Monty Hall tries to distract Robert. He leans into Robert's ear and says firmly, "Robert, how about THE BOX? THE BOX!"

"The box," Robert says. The box is on a table right in front of Robert, but he is looking at something beside it— something not there. A baby in an incubator. When Robert utters "the box," Monty wastes no time. Ceremoniously he opens the box. Revealed is a single pinecone, unusually large, undamaged, flawless—a perfect form. It's what Margie brought to trade.

Robert doesn't reach for it. He doesn't see it. Monty looks to Robert's counselor in an unspoken plea for help. The counselor comes forward, takes hold of Robert's left hand, and gives it a gentle tap. Robert opens his palm. With one quick motion, Robert's counselor removes the Juicy Fruit and places the pinecone in Robert's palm.

Robert's fingers wrap themselves around the pinecone and show that they comprehend the object they hold, even if his mind does not. His hand grasps with just the right tension: a solid hold, but not so hard as to bend a bristle. Then, while the face keeps staring at the invisible incubator—or the price sticker on a car it might buy—the hand draws the pinecone to the left ear and scratches across the bristles. Intently, Robert scratches and listens, and on tippy-toe allows himself to be led back to his cabinmates.

Margie beams. "He really likes it. Because it's so pretty, that's why."

Her voice is strong. Even proud.

Because we showered early in the day, there's time to relax before lights-out. Carole has gone across to wash her hair. Escaping the hot cubicle, Sue sits on Dolly's footlocker and cuts her toenails. My ears follow the conversation around me, but my eyes drift toward Sue. Like a kitten, I tend to follow movement, even the small movements of a young woman bending a leg, holding a foot, methodically clipping, three snips per toe.

I stretch my legs on my bed.

"That was a pretty bizarre scene," Sara says.

"What's wrong with Wi-llie?"

"Well, I think, probably—" She seems to consider carefully, making a medical diagnosis. "He's hideous!"

I sputter.

"You figured that out, huh?" She's almost smirking. "Well, then, you know about as much as I do. His bones are messed up. And his meat. And his metabolism. Watch him: He eats three plates of food at each meal, and still he's not much more than a skeleton. But ain't he, far and away, the ugliest thing you ever saw?"

There's no denying it.

"Ugly as sin," she continues, "but really a great guy. The best."

She rests her chin on her hand. "You know, I knew him for three years, and then I realized I never looked at him. I'd talk to him by the hour, but I never looked at him. Well, this really upset me, because I thought, if I won't look at him, who on earth will? So, that very minute, I looked him in the face, and I mean right straight at him. And—this is really funny—he hated it! He tried not to show it, but he was really squirming! So then, I told myself, to hell with this! I'm gonna look at him, and he and I are both gonna like it! And eventually we did. Now I almost think he's beautiful, because he looks like Willie and no one else in the world."

"Is he your boyfriend?"

"Oh, no. I'm not in the boyfriend business."

Carole returns in a huge sweatshirt and flip-flops, a big towel scrunched around her hair. "Sue, do we need to do the BM chart?"

"Yeah. Would you mind?" She's just finishing the first foot.

Carole gets a clipboard from the cubicle. She kneels

beside Sue and lays it on the footlocker, making *X*s on a form. Mary, yesterday. Dolly, today. Then she comes to me.

"Jean, have you had a BM since you've been here?"

I shake my head no. "Why do you want to know?" I want to ask. But she moves on before I can speak.

Sara explains. "They want everyone to have a BM every other day. If you don't, there'll be milk of magnesia at breakfast." She says it like the Wicked Witch of the West.

My face goes red. Laxatives give me cramps, and I hate going to the bathroom in a mad rush.

"Tell it not in Gath," she says quietly, "and publish it not in the streets of Askelon, but a while back, we all decided it's okay to lie on your BM charts. If you don't want a laxative, get a walkie-talkie to take you off the toilet in the morning, wipe you, and flush. Then you can report whatever you want to."

I shrug. As much as I hate laxatives, I hate to lie. Why don't the others seem bothered? They probably have BMs on record, real or fake. I want to change the subject.

"Sa-ra, why did-n't you go swim-ming?"

"Why should I? I'd rather spend my time drawing. I had to put 'Swimming only if requested' on my medical form, because otherwise they'd be after me to Overcome My Fear of the Water. Never mind that I'm not afraid. I used to swim, and I actually liked the ease of movement, the weightlessness. But it was too horrible when they pulled me out and all that gravity came crushing down."

Peggy Jo, the white walkie-talkie, is talking to Denise, the black epileptic. "Do you like this necklace? I'll trade for your book."

They are still making deals. I'm happy with the new Camp Courage T-shirt I won and lie back on the bed. Yvonne, the one-leg amputee, plops down in Sara's wheelchair, and they start a conversation. I'm mildly curious to know what they're saying. There are many things I'd like to know. What causes Denise's seizures? What's wrong with the white walkie-talkie? But I'm too tired to ask. I curl up and fall asleep even before lights-out.

The unexpected appearance of an ordinary object
may bring to consciousness what was previously
so familiar as to be unperceived.

As dawn comes, I am half awake and half asleep. Through the screened wall at my feet, I half see the sun rising.

On a distant ridge, pines stand in black silhouette against a pink and purple sky. It rained during the night. Thick clouds still hover over the horizon. As the sun moves up, silver beams penetrate the clouds to spotlight select trunks and boughs nearby, isolating them in dramatic contrast with the deep shade that hangs velvet-curtain-soft in the background. Pine needles touch the screens, and on them raindrop sequins sparkle. Every illuminated thing becomes magical and precious.

I am jolted into the kind of awareness that usually comes in dreams, an awareness of everything at once, everything so powerfully real that it seems impossible. I'm as awake as I've ever been in my life. I feel the light go through my eyeballs into my bloodstream. It warms the marrow of my bones.

My eyes move. Under the overhanging roof, the cabin's interior is illuminated by a muted, filtered glow. In that moment, I imagine that the light comes from inside me; it seems to be my own glow that blankets the sleeping forms around me. In seven uniform cots, those seven sleeping forms lie, each with its unique shape and size and position. If I want, I can, in an instant, call them all to life. I can, but I won't. Better to watch them sleep. As I watch them lying oblivious to my watching, they lose their distinctness. They become part of me. It is almost more than I can bear. I close my eyes.

The feeling has come without warning. It always does. And whenever it comes, it brings back the memory of the first time. The time I saw the termites. I lie still and let the memory overtake me.

It was early in my walking period. Cindy and I were playing in our backyard. "Girls, it looks like rain!" Mom called from the kitchen. Cindy raced inside. I turned around, my walker and braces clattering.

That's when I saw them, swarming right in front of me, just above my head. Termites. So marvelous. At the time, I didn't know why. Now I know. It was the light. It always is. The yard was in deep shadow, that ghastly gray-green shadow that comes just before a summer storm. But just as I saw the termites, a beam of purest white light traveled ninety-three million miles through a hole in the cloud to find them. In the brilliant light, innumerable wings glimmered silver and gold.

The movements of the tiny lights were unpredictable but ordered. They never collided. They never touched. But neither did they stray. In their swarm they held close, so close, held by the light maybe, or maybe by some kind of termite gravitational pull. It was a force that was way beyond my eight-year-old understanding. But whatever it was, it held me too.

Transfixed, I gripped my walker until I was near collapse. My mother called again. Just as she opened the door, the cloud moved and turned off the spotlight. I heard thunder and told my feet to take me inside.

"Jean, what got into you?" my mother asked cheerfully as my brace shoes scraped across the patio.

"No-thing," I said, and my mother lifted me up and carried me the last few steps into our house.

You can tell it's Sunday by the smell of pancake syrup. The big exhaust fans suck the breakfast fumes from the lodge and blow them out back, where we're all gathered for a worship service. A quartet of counselors leads the singing. "We are climbing Jacob's ladder."

I have a spot in the shade, but the sun is moving up, and I hope the service will be brief. Mr. Bob says a prayer. It's hot but still tolerable. Overall, the morning is going well. I've accomplished my main goal: persuading my bowels to extrude a few bullets into the toilet bowl. No need for milk of magnesia, or for lies. And this morning, no seizure to start the day. Denise is feeling good. Relief is definitely in the air along with the syrupy smell.

They sing "Kumbayah," and I watch the sign language that goes with the words. Then "Rock of Ages." And that's all. There's no sermon, no call to the spirit. Good. It's a simple Sunday morning routine—like having pancakes for breakfast and skipping cabin cleanup.

With a handful of campers I stay where I am and watch the chairs get folded. It's peaceful, relaxed, but Sara seems determined to stir something up.

"Rock of Ages," she bursts out in a hick twang, "cleft for me, lay-et me hiiide myself in thee." She leans forward and challenges us all. "I'll buy a Coke for anyone who can tell me what that means."

I turn my head to watch Margie carry two chairs away. I don't want to get into it.

"Well?" Sara asks.

"The Rock of A-ges," I say at last, "is God. Cleft means bro-ken."

"So. Let's see. We've been singing, 'God, broken for me, let me hide myself inside you?' Does this make sense? Am I missing something here?"

The others laugh.

"May-be you need to read the Bi-ble a lit-tle."

"You might be surprised, but I do. Parts of it, anyway. There are some great tales in it."

Back for more chairs, Margie claps her hands. "Tell us a Bible story!" She unfolds a chair and sits in it.

"Shall I?"

Willie lowers himself onto the grass right beside me. All I can see of him are those boulder knees and the top of his head. "Let's hear the story of Sara." The top of his head, covered with wavy brown hair, doesn't look bad at all.

"Okay." Sara pauses to look into each face and draws her breath, a little warm-up routine. "I'll tell you the story of a woman named Sara, like me. She married a man named Abraham. A very interesting man. He was rich, so all the relatives thought he was a great catch, and they lived in a beautiful house in a very old city—ancient even back then in ancient days. The city was called Ur. Ur was a very elegant and civilized place. The rich people there prayed to beautiful statues of bulls made out of gold and lapis lazuli." She turns to Margie. "That's a bright blue stone with flecks of gold."

Margie's eyes go big as her brain tries to make a picture of the gorgeous idol.

"Well, when Abraham was getting up in years, he went out to the country to see how his slaves were getting along with his livestock. When he came home, he told Sara he wouldn't pray to the bull anymore, because a burning bush had told him that It was the one true god."

"You mean the bush?" Margie asks.

"That's right. The bush claimed to be the one true god. But the bush wouldn't tell Abraham its name. When he asked, it said, 'I am that I am.' Well, Sara was okay about praying to Abraham's bush if that's what he wanted—it was all the same to her. But Abraham really went off the deep end. He couldn't stop obsessing about the bush. So one day he made a decision: He and Sara would sell their house in the city of Ur and go out into the country. They would wander around with the cows and sheep to be closer to the bush."

Wasn't it Moses who saw the bush? I'm not sure; I let Sara talk.

"The relatives told Sara that Abraham was clinically insane and she had no obligation to go along. But Sara decided to drop out with Abraham. Maybe she was bored in Ur. Maybe she didn't want to listen to everyone talk about her crazy husband and how the guy who'd looked so great wasn't such a catch after all. Maybe she worried about what would happen to him if she didn't go take care of him."

"May-be she loved him," I say.

"Could be," Willie agrees.

"Maybe." Sara obviously doesn't favor my theory. "I don't know why she went, but she did.

"They spent years wandering—all over nowhere. A couple of times, Abraham saw his bush again. Sara never saw it, but she stayed with him anyway. She stayed even when he got a slave woman pregnant, and even when he offered to give Sara—and I mean 'give' her in the Biblical sense—to another traveler. He did that twice, in fact, even after God sent an angel to tell him to stop it. Sara stayed, because by then she had no home to go back to. She had no children to take care of her.

"One day, when Sara was ninety years old, an angel of the Lord came to deliver a message from God. The angel told Sara she was going to have a baby, and be the Mother of Nations.

"Guess what Sara did then."

I don't know. We all look at one another. No one knows.

"She laughed. She laughed right in the face of a messenger of the Lord.

"Nine months later, the Lord got the last laugh. Or almost. Sara, age ninety-plus, gave birth to a baby boy. She named him Isaac. That was really the last laugh. In Hebrew, Isaac means 'we laugh.' I've always been pleased that I have that woman's name."

I look back and see that Carole has joined us. She is pushing a piece of wayward red hair behind her ear, squinting in the sun, laughing in her way, I think. "Willie, you know your cabin's out front looking for you?"

Sue stands with her feet firmly planted on the floor. She's in charge of indoor sports. "Okay, you two. Tell me what y'all want to play." The others are already playing games with one of the boys' cabins.

"Scrabble?" Sara asks me.

"You can play Scrabble at home," Sue says.

Sara scratches her head. "Is that a good reason not to play it here? Am I missing something?"

I shrug. Scrabble would be fun; we do play it at home, and I always impress everyone by keeping score in my head. But Scrabble isn't on the program. I look around at CPs and MRs throwing horseshoes in the general direction of the spike and lurching around the shuffleboard courts.

I say, "How a-bout putt-putt?" Dad and Cindy like to play, and sometimes when no one else is around, I take a swing myself. A little course is free.

"Oh, why not?" Sara rolls her eyes and Sue puts a club in her hands. With a parody of pro-golf precision, Sara lines up her stroke, limbers up her shoulders, and tap. . . . The ball rolls barely five inches. My turn. *Slam!* The ball flies from one end of the course to the other and ricochets back, ending up almost where it started.

"Whoa!" Sara says. "Now I'll tap mine around this little incline and approach the hole from the rear." The ball goes exactly as she says. Three inches. "Jean, dahling," she says, "we're just *perfectly* matched."

I whack, nowhere near the ball, but I succeed in breaking one of the plastic obstacles off the course. Sara says, "Nice work, Spazzo." I respond with a kick.

Her ball is in a crater. With the next stroke, it twitches but gains no ground whatsoever.

"Ve-ry good, Feeb!" It's all I can think of to say, but it gets us both laughing.

In tiny increments, she moves her ball out of the crater and eventually into the hole. When my ball goes in, it takes me completely by surprise. I'm also surprised to find I really want to win. All the excitement seems to be at the horse-shoe game, but Sara and I are actually competing. Her constant wisecracks make concentration impossible, but I don't need concentration, not the way I play. Finally I get stuck in a tight corner, and the game peters out. Worn out by exertion and laughter, we join the crowd at the horseshoe game.

It's Margie against a paraplegic boy. "How's she doing?" Sara asks.

Denise answers, "Just watch."

Limbering up for the toss, the boy throws his weight backward onto his big wheels. The casters pop up, and he rolls around on his back wheels.

"Look at that!" Sara says. "Popping wheelies. Paras think they're such hot stuff!"

He pops down and snarls, "Hey, I'm trying to throw."

"Trying. Okay. You're trying, and Margie's succeeding, right?"

"Sara!" Sue says severely.

"Please forgive me, so very sorry. I know you need your concentration."

I let a little squeal escape.

"Jean!" Sara copies Sue's stern voice. "We can have no inappropriate spazzing, do you hear? Our brother paraplegic NEEDS to concentrate."

I squeal again.

"Jean! How is he supposed to throw? How is he supposed to dazzle us with that world-famous para upper-body strength? Calm down, Jean. I said calm down." I try. Sort of. Not really.

He glowers, but obviously he's enjoying the attention. Finally he lands on all four wheels, takes a horseshoe, and rolls toward the spike. His powerful arm swings in a broad arc, nearly scraping the floor before turning upward again. Just before the top of the curve, he lets go. A decent toss. Real close. Now it's Yvonne who lets out a little squeal. Sara cuts a look at Yvonne and whispers to me, "You know, they say the paras may get the girls, but the quads keep them."

Margie takes her position. On the floor beside her feet there are four horseshoes. She squats down and takes one up and rises to throw, eyes fixed steady on the spike. *Clang.* A ringer! Cheers rise up. I go spastic: all four limbs jerk wild and free, and from my mouth comes a wild, free squeal.

Margie doesn't react. She's focused on the spike as she squats again and her strong hand takes an easy hold on a second horseshoe then lets go. *Clang.* It lands neatly on top of the other, wrapped around the spike. Then comes the third. *Clang!* We're in a frenzy, but Margie remains unmoved by any victory rush, undistracted by the racket we're making. The fourth lands. Another perfect toss. There are no horseshoes left.

I'm in the middle of a full-blown spaz attack, and I don't care. I don't care at all. At home I always try to act normal, and spaz attacks definitely aren't normal. Here, people understand. They know a spaz attack signals that I'm excited. They're excited too, so they squeal with me; some even spaz on purpose, if you can call that spazzing, and fool around making CP joy-sounds. Sue cuts them a look to make them stop copying me, but I like it.

I stay semispastic through lunch. Three times I choke on my food. I don't even try to calm down until rest period. I stretch my hot, aching legs and arms, but I'm too keyed up to sleep. A long spaz attack is like a full-body workout. As tired as I am, I'm not too tired to notice how happy I feel.

Instead of gathering in front of the lodge to wait for supper, we're taken out back. Sara surveys the scene and points to an empty card table on the far end of the field. "Over there." She speaks to Sue like she's in New York giving directions to a cabdriver.

Sue pushes her with one arm, and with the other pulls me across the grass. Tonight the kitchen staff, usually invisible, are working out in the open. Two men watch charcoal grills while women lay out cold food, pat hamburgers, and give orders. On the field, visiting young people are carrying things for the cooks and serving Cokes.

Sue parks us at the little table Sara has selected, far from the action. "Thanks, that's great." I half expect Sara to hand Sue a bill and tell her to keep the change. She waves Margie and ugly Willie over.

"There's no room for the Community Youths, now," she says.

"Yeah." Willie says, "Good move." He sniffs the charcoal smoke. "Yum, smells delicious."

"Damn," Sara says, "with the appetite you have, I bet a steaming pile of horseshit would smell delicious to you."

He may be smiling, but it's hard to tell. I notice one of the visitors, a cute guy a bit older than me, carrying an ice chest across the field. He looks sort of foreign, Italian maybe, or Spanish. Not too far away, a half dozen visitors are sitting on a blanket. I'd like to join them. I could get Margie to push me over; then I'd transfer out of my chair onto the blanket and say hello. But that would make Sara mad.

Willie and Sara talk. I brood. What gives Sara the right to run everything? Why does Willie go along? The two of them can talk nonstop for hours. They have everything in common. They love the same TV shows and books, and they hate the same people, including President Nixon.

"Now, Sara," Willie says, "you know the bombing's a secret. Top secret." His voice is transformed into Nixon's, but nothing can transform his hideous face. "Nobody knows about it. Nobody at all. Except, of course, the Cambodians. Why, er, they know. Er, all too well." He raises his twisted-skeleton arms and extends his fingers in a twisted parody of Nixon's V for Victory sign.

They trash various cabinet officers and senators. I don't get a lot of it, but Margie is giggling behind her hand like she understands. Maybe she's too simple to know that the talk is way above her head. Or maybe it's enough that Sara and Willie like her. They do like her. I don't quite get that either.

A cook yells, "Come and get it!"

Willie jumps to his feet. "What do y'all want? Some of everything?"

I nod.

"I'll take a cheeseburger with ketchup and pickles and lots of chips," Sara says. "This is the only decent meal we'll get around here."

Willie and Margie stand together in the food line. In a neat pink shorts suit, Margie takes her characteristic stance: sway-backed, hand over mouth, staring at feet. Willie stands facing Margie, his back to the crowd, in long pants for a change, and a Disneyland T-shirt. Did he have the nerve to show his face in the Land of Make Believe? I can't imagine them letting him in. Silence falls between

Sara and me. I concentrate on getting a better attitude. I might as well enjoy myself.

Margie and Willie are back with paper plates bending under the weight of the food. "Get a load of this!" He shoves half a hot dog into his mouth, and, chewing, heads back for drinks. Margie sits down to eat.

"What's so bad a-bout Nix-on?" I ask, and immediately wish I hadn't.

"What ain't bad about him?" Sara says. Margie laughs hard, maybe because Sara said *ain't*.

Willie is back with the drinks and sits beside me, turned away from all the activity. "So what have y'all been talking about?"

"Nixon," Margie says.

Willie holds a hot dog to my mouth. Oh, no. I'm supposed to take food from that twisted hand. My stomach goes queasy, but there's no choice. Sara can't feed me. Margie could, but she's too shy. No counselors are around; Sara arranged that. I don't want to insult Willie, so I put my mouth around the hot dog and chomp down, barely aware that he's started doing an imitation of Honorable State Senator and Camp Benefactor B. J. McNeill.

That first bite is the hardest. After that, I can manage, so long as I don't look at Willie stuffing his face. The hot dog tastes really good. That helps. I finally hear the story about the MR and the pie in the face at Talent Night. It was Senator McNeill, last year—not quite a direct hit but close enough, and he had no choice but to be a good sport. Willie offers me a potato chip. Another little agony. His fingers touch my lips, and the dry chip sticks in my throat. I swallow again. All right. All right. I take another bite and feel mustard and baked beans dribble down the corners of my mouth. He wipes my chin with a paper napkin. I hope the shudder doesn't show.

This ordeal is pushing all irritation and annoyance out of my mind. By the time I finish eating, I'm proud of myself for getting through it. I sit back and let Willie eat. I'm so relieved I don't even mind being separated from the normal youths from the community.

Willie and Sara are talking about old times. "Don't you miss Mr. Mann?" she asks.

"Oh, sure! Our camp director last year," he tells me. "He was this drill-sergeant type who thought we should 'rough it.'"

"Right! Us!"

"But you have to give Mr. Mann credit. He stuck to his guns. In the end, what it came down to was no radios."

"Not even for the moon landing."

"But the counselors smuggled 'em in. I'm not sure why. They didn't particularly like the moon landing; they were just as back-to-nature as Mr. Mann—"

"Although for different philosophical reasons. These are the Jesus Freaks we're talking about."

"Yeah. Maybe philosophy had something to do with their bringing in radios. The First Amendment or something."

"No, Willie. It was because Mr. Mann was a prick!"

He shakes his head. "Sara, please."

"Well, that's what they called him. The Prick."

He throws up his hands. "Okay, I won't argue. To get back at the Prick, the Jesus Freaks smuggled in radios, and thus we knew—"

"Thus?"

"Thus we knew that the astronauts made it! A small step—"

Sara interrupts. "Look at that guy. Robert. He still blows me away." Now dressed in green from hat to socks, aussie Robert is standing up and making those little circles in the air with his finger. Sara and Willie go silent.

I bet they're trying to figure out what he's doing. It hits me. "Next year, he'll do this." With my right index finger I jab at the air. Seven stabs.

Sara can't figure it out. "What?"

"Push-but-ton phone."

Two more times Willie goes through the line and comes back with plates piled high with hot dogs, hamburgers, slaw, potato salad, chips, corn on the cob, and water-melon. After all that, he goes back for two big slabs of cake. As he scrapes the crumbs, Sara swallows the last tiny bite of her cheeseburger.

"You're the only person who can keep up with me," he says.

"Yeah, hour for hour, I sure can. But you've eaten five times as much."

That is a smile on his face. I'm pretty sure.

He pats his stomach, and Margie gathers up the trash while at the other end of the field the visiting youths assemble on bleachers. The sun is low in the sky. Someone throws the switch to turn on a bank of yellow lights, and Mr. Bob stands at a microphone in front of the bleachers.

"Campers and counselors, most of you have met our guests, but I'm pleased to introduce them officially. They are the Sand Hills Community Youth Chorale, and they will provide the evening's entertainment. Welcome them, please."

Starting with "Shenandoah," they go through the standards that let a choir show its stuff. They're good, every bit as good as our glee club at Crosstown High. The sky goes pale pink and orange, then red and purple, then deep blue.

The choir director speaks. "We thank you for welcoming us into your midst. You have touched us and warmed our hearts. We leave you with this inspiring song from *Man of La Mancha*."

Sara turns to Willie, "Oh God, here it comes!"

"Yep, we couldn't escape."

"The Ideal Cripple's Code of Conduct," Sara groans. Margie covers her face with both hands.

The choir sings "The Impossible Dream." Willie and Sara mouth the words:

> *To fight the unbeatable foe.*
> *To bear with unbearable sorrow.*

Their lip-sync is clearly a standard routine, employing dramatic gestures from the ham actor's standard bag of tricks—hands over hearts, terrified nail biting, defiant fist raising. With stern looks, counselors discourage the mirth that spreads, inappropriately, from group to group. But they keep at it:

> *To right the unrightable wrong.*
> *To love, pure and chaste from afar.*
> *To try when your arms are too weary—*

By the time Willie stands on tip-toe to reach for the unreachable star, Willie, Sara, and Margie have reached a state of high hilarity. I just can't see what's so funny.

Now they're calm, still apparently waiting for something.

> *And the world will be better for this.*
> *That one man—*

Willie's cue. He stands up—

Scorned and covered with scars . . .

He half salutes and half bows, like a celebrity being recognized in the audience of *The Ed Sullivan Show*. ("Now appearing on Broadway, one man, scorned and covered with scars.")

Sara's wiping her eyes with a crumpled napkin. "Wait till you see Senator B. J. McNeill do that celebrity wave. Willie's got it perfect."

The song continues

. . . with his last ounce of COURAGE . . .

But the ending is lost. The laughter has become hysterical. Sara's red-faced, choking, as close to a spaz attack as she can get. Again I wish they hadn't dragged me to this table.

Mr. Bob looks to us with the sternest disapproval before turning to the choir. "Encore."

The choirmaster raises his arms.

"What'll it be, do you think?" Sara asks.

"What the World Needs Now Is Love, Sweet Love," Margie whispers. Sara nods and Willie gives Margie an appreciative poke on the back.

No. It isn't "What the World Needs Now." With the

first notes, I think I see Willie's face light up with devilish mirth. "Look out."

"Oh, shit, I should've known." Sara rests her chin on the table like a long-suffering tired old hound.

"When you walk through a storm . . ." This time they listen silently, waiting, waiting for something that doesn't come until the big ending.

"WALK ON, WALK ON, with hope in your heart, and . . ."

Willie takes Sara's hands and my hands and joins them in his own. With death-sentence solemnity, he speaks the next line: "You'll never walk alone."

Sara ham-acts a face of great distress, a face hearing very bad news for the first time.

Willie sings loud, right in our faces. "You'll NEVER WALK alone!"

I laugh.

The other routine annoyed me, but this one—I have to laugh. I have to laugh because there's no way to keep calm with that hideous face singing right into mine, that weird knobby leathery hand so alive, so warm, squeezing mine. But I laugh too, to express something I'm just beginning to feel: that walking is something you can mock. Not walking as an ordinary means of getting around, but Walking as a big dramatic idea, Walking as a metaphor for strivings of all kinds. When I gave up my childhood struggle to walk, it felt like a failure of something much greater—a failure of courage, of character, of faith. Yesterday Sara suggested that walking might be a matter of choice. Today it's a joke. A joke so funny I can't stop laughing.

I laugh through the ripple of applause for the chorus, laugh through the dispersal of the herd, and laugh as we move toward the cabin. I barely notice that Carole is particularly nonplussed and Sue is looking daggers at Sara.

We stop outside the cabin. Sara and I are parked on the path and Sue sits opposite us on a bench. It's night now. A big light shines right in Sue's face. She leans forward and looks at Sara. "Listen. We need to talk about your inappropriate behavior tonight—"

"Oh? Do we?"

"Yes. We do. That group came out to entertain us. It was rude to make fun of them."

I feel a little sorry, now, but anger sparks in Sara's eyes. "Please. We have to laugh."

"Sara, you—"

"I mean, seriously, 'The Impossible Dream.' We hear it here every year, and it's on every telethon, and it haunts us in crippled school. Someone decided it was an appropriate song to inspire crippled folks, and I'm fed up with it. If you tell me I can't laugh—"

"It's just a popular song."

"Not when they sing it to us. Then it's a put-down; it says we don't have a real life and certainly not a real future, so we're supposed to retreat into dreams, and not nice pleasant dreams but pathetic impossible dreams. Like, 'Someday there may be a cure,' 'God bless us every one,' 'I'm writing a novella.'"

For a moment, she drops her head and sits in silence. When she looks out again, it's like I can see pain flare from her face, loop around the three of us, whip past the going-to-bed noises coming from the cabins. Sue hunches down, as if to escape the defiance in that pain and then leans forward, determined to try once more.

"Sara, you—"

"They want us to live in pathetic fantasy, so they can thank God they're not like us. And, anyway, who the hell do they think they are, these dumb Norm-visiting Philistines? What do they know about Walking Through Storms? It's shit."

"Watch your language," Sue says sharply. "Think about them. They deserve basic courtesy. They meant well."

"Then so much the worse. They're dumb passive channels for every dumb idea this society has about Crips. Every stereotype. It's like we're black or something, considering the amount of abuse and prejudice we get thrown at us. I've had enough impossible dreaming."

"Come on, Sara. You must know that—some people need their illusions."

Sara's anger is controlled, focused, like a welder's torch. "Sue, you don't understand. You never will. You've counseled us about our terribly inappropriate behavior, okay? That's all anyone can ask. Let's go inside."

For a moment more we sit, and Sara's anger also lingers, like a living presence. Now I wish Sue had just let her laugh. Let us laugh. Sue glances up at the night sky, then finger-combs her hair and shakes her pageboy back into its perfect wave. She stands up tall and straight and takes us inside to get ready for bed.

After taps, I lie in bed and think Sara is an unusual person. Some of her peculiarities are obvious, of course, the second you look at her, the minute you hear her arch and irritating talk. Others I'm just beginning to see. At the cookout, I saw one thing. She laughs. She can laugh at anything, at anyone, no matter what message they bring, no matter by what power sent. Now I know the laughter is serious. Angry. Painful. Was it that way for the other Sara, when she laughed at the messenger of the Lord?

I drift in and out of sleep, replaying in my mind fragments from the day that has ended. The first light of dawn. Spazzing: the clang of Margie's horseshoes. We laugh: You'll never walk alone. I'll never walk alone. Never.

My mind drifts away from this place, this time. My PT is telling me, "You can do it if you try." I am in Sunday school: "You can do it if you believe." I see Jesus cleansing lepers, giving sight to the blind, making the lame walk. He heals them all and then leaves them behind. In the fresh air of the Swiss Alps, the orphan girl Heidi tells her crippled cousin, Clara, "You can do it; just try." In the fresh air of a secret garden, another orphan girl, another crippled cousin: "You can do it; just try." As a child I loved these stories; they speak to the fundamental optimism of childhood. Part of me still believes them, or wants to. But now I yearn for a Bible story about a cripple who isn't cured.

Outside in the night, crickets chirp. I've heard the sound all my life, but for the rest of my life I will associate it with Camp Courage. That night, and in other nights to come, the crickets sing, "Isaac, Isaac, Isaac."

We laugh.

The line creates no bounds, has no perimeter,
no area, no outside, no inside. It is
without form and therefore infinite.

On the first note of reveille, I stretch and hope my bathing suit is dry. Swimming is right after cabin cleanup. I hope we'll have orange juice with breakfast. I'm thirsty.

The others stir around me. I watch Margie rub her eyes with the back of her hand, Yvonne strap on her plastic leg, Denise and Peggy Jo head to the bathroom. Mary starts another day of eyebrow tapping. Across the room lies Dolly, possibly dreaming of Johnny Carson. And beside me is Sara, still sleeping, sleeping still, almost as still as death.

"Rise and shine!" Sue calls.

"Morning, everyone," Carole says.

This is how my days start now. I've become subject to a routine that has made me part of this place, has merged me with the others, and now governs our collective movements. In an orderly flow, we circulate through paths; we pulse up and down hills with regular rhythms and with little thought of other places we might be. For me, there's little thought of that oddly empty home in Crosstown, that family with one person missing, strangely encamped on the beach. Four days ago, that home and that family made up my world. But now this is my place.

It's only the second time I've watched people drop body parts on the sand by the lake, but now there's no need to gawk. A dwarf boy ambles into the water in electric blue swimming trunks. A thalidomide girl holds sunglasses in her right flipper while a counselor daubs suntan lotion on her nose. In the deep water, the floating quad is attached by a tube to a floating plastic bag half full of amber urine. Up on the dock, Sara sits. She'd rather fry in the sun than face the moment when the water lets go and gravity comes crushing down. All of this is mildly interesting.

I hand myself over to the cool, thick water and feel it lift me up. Holding me down is gravity. I float across the plane of the lake's surface, comfortable in my own proper orbit. To me, gravity is a good old friend.

In a stuffy clearing in deep shade, Margie sings softly to herself. "Old Mary Mack, Mack, Mack, all dressed in black, black, black . . ." Sara starts a pastel sketch, and I think about what's next.

Horseback riding is no problem for the walkie-talkies;

they're out now. Yvonne manages very well with her artificial leg. And Margie, singing her childish song:

She went upstairs, stairs, stairs
To make her bed, bed, bed
and bumped her head, head, head—

She'll be afraid at first, but both horses are old and slow. For me, the problem won't be riding itself—I can keep my seat in my uncle's motor boat, even bouncing over a wake—but getting on the saddle. There are three counselors on duty: a girl counselor, the guy who played Monty Hall, and Carole. I guess somehow they will get me on.

Margie's song stops abruptly. The riders are back.

"You want to be next?" Monty Hall asks Dolly.

"I'm not sure I have time. I really need to work on my novella. It's really RISQUÉ—"

"Lovely lady, ride a few minutes with me and your writing will be all the better."

In reply, she blabs something, who can tell whether consenting or what? They push her toward the barn and open a gate. Now I see. There's a ramped platform that brings wheelchairs up to saddle-height. Monty gets on the horse first. When they unlatch Dolly from her chair, it takes all three to catch her bolting body and stuff it onto the saddle in front of Monty.

"Hang on tiiiiight!" she shrieks. Legs and arms spring

out like four scared rattlesnakes striking at the four winds. Monty is big but no athlete. It takes all his strength to hold back her writhing and keep her from hitting the ground and bringing him down too. I look to Sara for a pertinent comment, but she keeps her eyes down on her drawing.

Monty's breathing hard. "I'm gonna need both of you. One on each side. Be ready. She could go either way." Sweat rolls from his curly hair down his dusty red face.

"We'll be within hollering distance, okay?" Carole says. "Peggy Jo, can you please keep an eye on Mary? On everyone?"

"Sure, we'll be fine."

They disappear into the woods. Through the trees we hear the usual prattle about the sexy steamy risqué work-in-progress.

I ask Sara, "Will they have to hold you on?"

"I don't ride."

We sit and wait. Peggy Jo walks aussie Mary around the clearing. I wonder what's wrong with Peggy Jo, the white walkie-talkie. I search for distinguishing physical characteristics. She's of average height, average build, with medium brown chin-length hair. An ordinary face, just slightly thin, with a nose no pointier than most. Margie is singing again, on a new tack.

"Mary had a lil-ole lamb, lil-ole lamb, lil-ole lamb. Mary had a lil-ole lamb—The BIBLE—TELLS ME—SO!"

Sara says it almost prayerfully: "Lamb of God! Sweet Jesus!"

They come back with Dolly a bigger mess than ever: legs flying apart, back flat on the saddle, head spazzing all over Monty's ample lap. Monty has a good lock on her, but it's doubtful that her mangled shirt and shorts can hold up to the pressure for long. Huffing and yelling, they manage to get her back in her chair and strapped down. Through it all, the blabbing never stops.

Monty leans on the fence. Still winded, he asks Sara, "Ready for a ride?"

"Thank you, no. I'll pass."

"Come on," Monty's assistant says. "Don't be afraid!"

"It's not that I'm afraid," Sara says frostily. "It's that I don't like to ride."

"Have you ever tried it?" Monty asks. "Nooo? You can't know for sure you don't like it, unless you try."

"Rick. Get real."

Carole has found a stash of bobby pins in her hip pocket and is at work repairing her ponytail. "How can you be so sure? I mean, so sure?"

"For God's sake, any of us could name a zillion things we don't like, without actually trying them. Give me a little credit."

Carole gives up the fight with both Sara and her hair. "Jean, what about you? You game?"

I nod. I'm more nervous than I want to admit, but Carole is really sweet. No need to give her a hard time. I'm rolled up to the platform, and she helps me to my feet. I turn and sit down, and then Monty grabs my leg and lifts it over. No problem.

"Can you ride on your own?" I check my balance and nod yes.

The stable smells remind me of my grandfather's farm. Monty mounts the other horse and leads my horse to the trail. I soon feel comfortable enough to reach out and take the reins from him. Slow and easy, the horse proceeds over the path. As an experiment, I pull back on the reins. The horse stops.

That's power. Horse power.

A nudge from Monty makes my horse move forward. Beside me, Monty's long slow stride matches my pace. His head and mine are bobbing along at the same level, more or less. It's like we're two walking people, a pair of walking friends, strolling side by side. If I need help, Monty's here, but I'm not depending on him. I'm not depending on anyone. Well, except the horse, but to the horse I am master. That's what the big animal believes and by believing makes it so.

Easily we pass across sand that would have swallowed my casters. We step over roots and bramble. My body takes up the gentle side-to-side wobble that makes up a gait. I haven't felt that rhythm, haven't moved with the rhythm of walking, since I was little enough to be carried in my parents' arms.

I want to smile, but I hold back. If I smile, I'll get happier. If I get too happy, I'll lose control.

The woods thicken and the trail narrows. Monty falls behind, and I lead us onward, through the lush air the plants have exhaled. Here, tree trunks are a deep rich color I don't have a name for, not quite brown, not quite gray, almost purple. Pine needles glisten black. I smell the mold working on the old growth, returning it to the earth. A dove coos.

Am I taking more time than the others did? Am I going deeper into the woods? I don't care. I want to go as far as the trail and the horse can take me, to breathe this air and make it part of me. I want to know what these woods are like. A low branch reaches out to scrape my arm and pine needles tickle my skin.

Monty's voice calls from behind, "We'd better head back."

In the cabin, Peggy Jo looks up from the letter she's writing. "Jean, you looked great on that horse."

I grin.

"I loved being up there. I felt so independent." Peggy Jo says.

"Me too." I'm surprised she feels the same way. I turn to Sara. "I'm sorry you didn't go rid-ing. It was great."

She folds the letter she's written. "Yeah, for you. You can really ride. But I can't sit up on a saddle. Even if they could manage to get me up there without twisting me into complete quadhood, I just don't see any need to bounce around on a hot smelly beast. Maybe it turns Dolly on, but different strokes for different folks, you know. For me, maybe independence comes from refusing to be put on the horse."

"You don't ride. You don't swim. If you don't like the ac-ti-vi-ties, why have you come to camp for eight years?"

"Mercy! If I had to like the activities, I'd have nowhere to go. All over the crippled world, the activities are weird. I come because my family needs a vacation from me. And I need to be with my people. The Crip Nation."

I snort.

She puts the letter in an envelope and writes the return address: Mary Rodgers, c/o Camp Courage. Mary the eyebrow tapper. She addresses it to Miss Eva Jones at Butner.

"How did you know who to write?" I ask.

Sara whispers, "Took a peek at her file."

"I have to write a thank-you letter to the man who paid my way to camp," Yvonne moans. "I don't know what to say!"

"Me neither!" Peggy Jo says.

"Aw, come on, people!" Sara says, "What's the big deal? 'Dear whoever—'"

"Senator McNeill," Yvonne says.

"Oh, but of course, the Great Benefactor himself. 'I am'—how old?"

"Sixteen."

"Okay, 'I am a sixteen-year-old with one leg amputated from—'"

"Lumberton."

"'Without your help, I could not afford to go to camp. I am enjoying it very much, especially swimming. Thank you.' Exclamation point."

Peggy Jo laughs. "I'm going to write the same letter, pretty much." She labors over it. "This doesn't look right. Asthma is *a-s-t-h-m-a*, right?"

"Yes, I think so," Sara says. "So is that what you've got?"

Peggy Jo nods.

"But you do fine in the air around here. Even at the stables." She scrunches up her nose remembering a bad smell.

"Yeah, I haven't had a severe attack for over four years. But it was bad when I was little. After my third time in the hospital, they told my parents to put me in Crip school. By the time my asthma got better, I was two grades behind. I didn't want to go back to Norm school and be a dummy so I stayed in Crip school. When you go to Crip school, you go to Crip camp in the summer. So here I am."

"Hey, don't worry," Sara declares. "Once a Crip, always a Crip."

"Did-n't you miss the o-ther kids when you left the nor-mal school?"

"Maybe at first. But in a way it was good. At Norm school I was the sick girl. At Crip school I'm the one who can do the most."

"And be the helper for everyone else, I bet," Sara says.

"I guess so. I like to help out."

"I like that too," Yvonne says, "and I like being where no one cares about this." She taps her plastic leg. "We have one Crip class and one MR class in a regular school. We're on one end of this hall, and we come in through the side door and whatnot."

"Do y'all mix up with the Norms at recess?" Sara asks.

Yvonne scrunches up her round face, tan like her frizzy hair. "No, we have a little side yard and there are bushes between our yard and theirs. Sometimes they peek at us through the bushes. They think we're weird."

"But you think they're weird too, right?" Sara seems to have heard it all before.

"Well, yeah! They are weird! In our yard we all sit around and talk—"

"Like civilized people," Sara says.

"Right! And when we peek through the bushes, we see them just running around, chasing one another—"

"Savages!" Peggy Jo says.

"Oh," Sara says, "I almost forgot. I'm supposed to do a survey before the Soviet meeting."

Sue's voice comes from behind the cubicle: "You mean the Camper Council."

"What's a Soviet?" Margie asks.

"A Soviet is an organization of deputies elected by the people to agitate on their behalf with the people in charge."

"Like the Camper Council!" Margie claps.

"Actually, the Soviets should be in charge, but that hasn't happened in any existing system. And it sure hasn't happened here. Our Soviet has no real power."

"Well, it's still an honor to be a member," Peggy Jo says.

"What does the Soviet do?" Margie asks shyly.

"For pity's sake, Sara!" Sue walks out of the cubicle. "You've got Margie using that word. Cut it out."

"Well, Margie, according to Fearless Leader Bob, our sole function is to make one decision for the people. We are to go through a stack of catalogues and pick a movie to watch. Not exactly a dictatorship of the proletariat, is it?"

"Naw," Margie says. They all shake their heads. I can't believe it.

Sara continues. "They're all old movies, but some of them are good. The boys are pushing for violence—John Wayne—and the girls want sex, or at least a love story. So far I've managed to hold back the Duke, but it looks like an impasse. So we recessed to poll our constituents." Eyes went blank. "I mean, to ask what y'all think."

"Co-me-dy?" I propose.

Heads nod all around.

"That's it!" Sara says. "Comedy, the common ground for boys, girls, MRs, aussies, and us Brains."

"Time to head up for supper," Sue says.

Carole pushes Sara outside, and Sue sits down to talk to the rest of us. "Listen. Y'all need to stop letting Sara influence you so much. Soviets are un-American. Communist. She's making a mockery of the men fighting in Vietnam. And she knows it."

I feel like telling Sue not to take Sara so seriously. She's just fooling around. And anyway, even if she manages to indoctrinate all the campers at Camp Courage it won't exactly hamper the war effort. We're a long way from the fighting. I'd be surprised if anyone out there even knows we exist.

"Can you look after our girls?" Sue asks another girl counselor. "We've got one who flat refused to let us put her in party clothes before supper, and now we've got to take her back. It's a two-person job too."

Aside from Dolly, we're all here in party clothes. I'm wearing my bell-bottom jeans and a white ruffled blouse I borrowed from Peggy Jo. The crisp new denim seems strange with the soft polyester satin, but they say it looks good. I think they're right.

"Y'all be good. We'll be right back." Sue says. She and Carole leave with Dolly.

We wait outside and I listen to the sounds coming

through the screens. Counselors hollering, tables and chairs being stacked, stuff scraping across the floor. A staple gun. They're getting ready for the dance. I listen for the Soviet meeting that's going on in a corner. I recognize Sara's voice, harping on about something, and then Willie's voice, sounding agreeable, but I can't make out the words.

The screen door opens and the Soviet members file out. Pushing Sara, Willie stops just outside the door and raises his lumpy fist. "We're victorious!"

Sara announces, "Comrades, it's *Horse Feathers*! A victory for Marxism! Marx Brothers, that is." She's still wearing the rumpled Mexican dress she's worn all day and hasn't even combed her sweaty hair.

We hear a guy call from inside, and a stampede is underway even before the door opens.

We don't exactly thunder; thunder was never so varied a noise. We yell, squeal, howl, and spaz. Walkers clatter, and leg braces squeak. Rubber crutch tips thud on the concrete stoop. Angling for position at the door, the para sideswipes the quad; the chrome rims of their big wheels clang. "Head 'em up! Move 'em in!"

Once past the bottleneck of the door, we reconstitute ourselves; from the formless mass, clusters of boys and clusters of girls congeal on the edges of the dance floor, with a little coed cluster at the punch bowl. I cluster with Denise and Margie.

Half the yellow bug lights go off, and the rest glow gold and rosy behind white and red Japanese lanterns. Crepe paper streamers blow in front of the fans. It's quite an effect.

The music starts: "One o'clock, two o'clock, three o'clock rock—"

Right away walkie-talkies are out on the floor with some of the nervier Crips. The para pops two wheelies in front of a girl counselor. She does the swim, and he starts the monkey. She leans on his armrest and wobbles him in time to the music. He should still be smarting from his humiliating horseshoe defeat, but he looks like he's having a great time, pumping those big arms while she holds her nose and dips.

Willie leans on my armrest and watches Sara and Yvonne talking on the other side of the room.

"So what's she up to?" he asks me.

"What?"

"Sara. Look how she's got Yvonne all wrapped up in some deep discussion. Don't you see? Looks like she's got one of her schemes going. What's she planning for Talent Night?"

"I don't know."

"Hmm. You really don't know, do you? She must be running it on a need-to-know basis."

I don't know what he's talking about. I don't say anything.

The next song starts, and counselors fan out to pull campers onto the dance floor. A counselor invites Margie to dance, but she looks like she might split in two with embarrassment and actually hides behind me. The guy shrugs and turns to Denise. "What about you?"

"Well. Okay, thanks," she says politely after just a moment's hesitation. He offers his hand; she doesn't take it.

Willie and I watch them dance. The guy is blond and very tan, like a surfer. Denise, only a shade or two darker, looks nice in a white cotton shirt and baby blue skirt and a little matching blue hairbow. Denise can really dance— and why not? Her body works perfectly well, until an electrical surge blows it out of whack. They look just like a normal couple.

In a way, at least.

I think of my family. They'd be shocked. My grandma would nearly die; she's an old-time Baptist and thinks all dancing is sinful. My parents aren't like that, but they say it's a sin to mix the races. I don't know. I guess I've never really needed to have an opinion: the only black people I've known until now, the people who work at my school, are married to each other. Now that I think about it, I guess mixing the races might not be a sin exactly, but it is asking for trouble. In most places, at least. Apparently here it's okay.

My eyes wander around the dance floor. The quad makes wide circles in his power chair, swooping around a girl counselor like a hawk over its prey. He pulls in close and makes tight little figures. She takes his withered hand, then presses her cheek to his, right beside his mouth controls. She touches him where he can feel it.

The guy is back with Denise. He approaches me with a nice open face. "May I have this dance?"

By now I've seen several varieties of wheelchair dancing and know what's expected. "De-light-ed," I say and slap my brakes loose. He holds my hand in a strong, warm grip and walks onto the dance floor. My chair glides easily on the linoleum floor; Dad keeps my bearings clean and my axles well-oiled.

Good. It's beach music. As soon as he takes his stance, I know he's an expert shagger. Like my parents. Mom's voice pops into my head. "Back when we were kids, your daddy and I used to go to the beach with the Baptist Youth and—now don't tell Grandma 'cause she'd kill us both—but at night we'd sneak off to the bars and shag with the college kids." On the living room carpet, Mom demonstrated the steps. I like to think about my parents, young, in love, and wilder than they are now.

I grin at the boy. "I love this mu-sic." I say it too loud.

"Me too." He steps close to me, wraps his fingers around mine. I let my hand squeeze back. He takes my other hand. Joined to me on both sides, he leans left and right, steps right and left, in a flat-footed shuffle that is relaxed and lazy like he's stepping on sand. He steps back.

I stiffen my arm and touch the floor with my toes to push my casters backward. He bends a knee and steps in; I pull in fast enough to make a breeze. Following his lead, I move forward, backward, side-to-side. I bob my head and shoulders. I am shagging. Not smooth, not elegant, not entirely cool, but shagging. I'm shagging with a guy with sun-bleached hair and nice brown legs under frayed cut-off jeans.

"Hey, that was great!" he says when the music stops. I can smell a hint of fresh sweat.

I feel pleasantly warm, a little sticky under the silky blouse. "Thanks. I had fun. I ne-ver shagged be-fore."

I can tell he doesn't understand. I gesture for him to push me to where Sara is now sitting alone. Yvonne and the para are out together, so busy talking and flirting that they're not doing much dancing.

"You okay here?" the surfer guy asks pleasantly.

I nod yes. He's gone.

"Hey, Spazzo," Sara says, "I was watching you out there. You got style, sure enough."

I laugh. I wonder if he'll ask me again. I liked moving with him, feeling his hands. I want to talk to him, maybe in a quieter place. I could ask if he learned to dance like that at Wrightsville Beach.

Willie comes up from behind and startles me. "I've waited eight years." Dramatically, he takes Sara's hand. "Is this the night?"

"Nope, not this night or any night. You know I don't dance." She grunts and frees her hand from his bent grip.

"Whatsa matter? You a lesbian?"

I am horrified.

"You males are such conceited assholes," Sara says with no anger at all. "A girl rejects you and you figure there's something wrong with her. Have you ever considered that there might be another explanation, for example the very likely possibility that you are the ugliest guy in the two Carolinas, maybe even in the thirteen original states?"

Willie pantomimes being stabbed in the stomach. Wincing, his face becomes even more hideous. "Oh woe, such is my lot! Scorned and covered with scars!" His voice sounds amused.

"Yeah, that's about the size of it, ain't it? Now get your butt and your last ounce of courage over to some girl counselor and ask her to dance. They get paid to buck up the delicate egos of guys like you."

He gives her a gentle poke on the arm and goes off and does her bidding. Dancing with a pretty girl counselor, he looks back at us and winks a fish eye.

For once, Sara is in no mood to talk. In silence, we watch the dancing. I notice the counselors acting as chaperones, making sure no one sneaks away or goes too far. Just like a normal dance. But at the same time, something isn't right.

A girl counselor dances close to an MR man, rubbing

her body against his as she jerks with the beat. Moving with her, he leans into her and reaches out to squeeze her behind. She pulls back, yanks his hand away, and shakes a disapproving finger at him. He drops his arms and his head. That's okay, I forgive you, she seems to say, and within seconds she's on him again. But now he keeps his arms down and doesn't even look at her.

Other counselors are just as bad. A perky girl counselor has set herself on the lap of a CP guy. Moving with the music, she teases at his face with her breasts, coming as close as she can come without actual touching. She must know that the slightest spasm would have him all over her—she must know it takes all his will to maintain that tiny distance between them—but she keeps up the torturous dance. He manages to hold back.

"Sara, why do the coun-se-lors act like that?"

"I wish I knew." She almost yells over the music. "I try to figure it out, and I keep changing my mind. It's obvious that something funny is going on. These counselors are mostly kids with pretty conservative morals, and you notice they don't have public foreplay with one another. Just with us. I don't get it." A male counselor is slow-dancing with the blind girl. He hoists her up by her buttocks and wraps her legs around his hips.

The music gets softer, and Sara lowers her voice. "At times I think they don't know what they're doing. They think we're children, or puppies, or sexless beings from outer space. They don't realize that, whatever else is wrong with us, we all—even the quads and paras and the Butner people who've been sterilized—all of us are capable of being aroused. At other times, I think, They have to know! They have to know what they're doing. It's so obvious.

"So, then, maybe they do it for the same reason they do almost everything. They think we need it. It's therapy. Just another facet of the whole Camp Courage mission to provide freaks with 'normal experiences.' Now, I'm no judge of Normal, I know, but this don't look like Normal to me." She laughs a laugh that leaves me cold.

"So, then, there's a third possibility. Maybe—they like it. Maybe these Norm kids get their kicks from rubbing up against cripples, epileptics, MRs, aussies, and every kind of freak. They know they're in control; each contact reinforces their dominance, their perfect able-bodied superiority. It's the special thrill of laying hands on lepers. It's how they know they're divine. Teasing freaks might just be a turn-on they don't get anywhere else."

I can't make up my mind either. That MR guy is standing like a folded-up ironing board with that girl counselor all over him. He is being so good, so passive, that she wraps her arms around his neck and presses her breasts against his chest. She pushes her hips, hard, against his groin. My experience is very limited, but I can tell the MR man is getting pretty hot. I'm not sure about the girl counselor.

Some of the campers, the ones with their heads screwed

on right, pull back. It kills me. They're trying to be polite. Some counselors take a hint; others don't. I see campers cringe beneath kisses they're powerless to resist. A few counselors act right. That surfer guy, for one, seems to know how to have fun without going over the line. But no one, not even the surfer guy, seems to disapprove of those who go too far. It is clearly acceptable at Camp Courage to tease Freaks.

Sara speaks again, so softly I can barely hear her over the music. "You know, the crazy thing is not just that I can't figure out why they do it, but I can't even decide what's worse. To be so misunderstood that they don't know we're sexual? To be thought so pitiful as to need this kind of therapy? Or to be exploited for their kicks? Can you tell me what's worse?"

I shrug. How can I know, when Sara, who has an answer, an analysis, for everything, doesn't know? I stare at Sara's feet dangling in dusty sandals.

The music stops, and the ceiling lights flash off and on. I look up to see Sue at the light switch, holding the door open. "Look out, everyone! She's here, all dolled up." Through the door comes Dolly, with Carole behind her pushing. I had forgotten all about them, but now I'm almost ill.

"WHO'S GONNA DANCE WITH ME FIRST?" Dolly squeals at the rafters. They've dressed her in a maxi skirt, slit up to the hip. Her drawn-up legs stick out of the slit entirely, leaving the skirt flapping limp behind them.

High-heeled shoes are taped to her feet. I can smell perfume across the room.

"There, you see?" Sara says icily, "The impossible dreamer. That's what they really want from us."

Boy counselors crowd around her.

Hello, Dolly.

"Now that Dolly's here," Sue says, "none of us girls will get any attention!" Carole adjusts Dolly's thin peasant blouse that has fallen off one shoulder. Three strings of love beads hang lopsided around the opposite breast. She's wearing green eye shadow, lots of blush, and frosted pink lipstick that's already smeared. Again the blouse falls off Dolly's shoulder. Again Carole reaches for it, but then holds back, maybe realizing that her efforts may be not only futile but also unwanted.

The boy counselors try to outdo one another in outrageous flattery.

"Look at that sexpot!"

"Man, she's really hot!"

"I can't stand it! Yow!"

I search for a hint of sarcasm but find none.

One sweaty guy crouches beside Dolly and whispers in her ear. Long sentences. He whispers until she howls, and, as she howls, she writhes against the belts that hold her in her chair. I'm sure I am blushing. It looks like she's having sex all by herself, with no touching required. Maybe this is what they want. They're certainly encouraging it.

I need something to do. I have to stop watching. I am afraid the surfer guy will get into the scene around Dolly, and that would make me crazy. When a walkie-talkie guy asks me to dance, I nod yes right away, without even sizing him up. I jerk and jerk to rock 'n' roll. CP makes it easy. I clench my fists. I don't want this guy to take my hand. I don't want him to touch me. I don't want any of them to touch me right now.

He pushes me back to Sara and asks her to dance. Her refusal allows no argument, and he goes away. Fine.

"You ne-ver dance?"

"Not in eight years in this place. That's a record."

"Do you think I should say no?"

"I don't know. I guess there's no harm. Just don't let them mess with your mind."

The music changes to rhythm and blues, and I wonder what do you do to keep people from messing with your mind. But before I can come up with an answer, the music starts to draw me in.

One bass guitar, one lone bass guitar, repeats five notes, less than a tune, over and over again. As though called by the bass, black counselors and black walkie-talkies fall in line on the floor. Holding hands, Denise and Margie take places at the end, and all seven brown bodies start bobbing up and down. The bobbing continues, and the bass continues, continues until it is almost too much, those five notes throbbing like an aching tooth.

When the first drum comes in, it feels like freedom, a door opening to release the song. On cue, a giggling girl bursts through the kitchen door, dragging an old cook by the apron. The drums hammer in counterpoint, and the older woman breaks loose and makes a run for the kitchen. A girl counselor falls out of the line and makes a joyful tackle, just as the drums and the bass shift into a new pattern. The other black people are laughing, but the line holds tight.

"It's an African thing," Sara says knowingly. I don't need her to tell me that. The white people have left the floor.

After making them force her into the line, the old cook slowly straightens her back and removes her apron. The others take a step back, deferring to her as leader. She stands. Listening. Listening to that vamp that seems to have no end. The others stand. Waiting. The guitars come in. Reed-thin, the woman sways. The line sways like grass in a warm summer breeze. The sax comes in, and the voices. The tempo jumps to a higher level. My heart jumps up, but the cook drops down, bending her knees deep. The line follows. She steps. The line steps.

The dance is serious business. Under her black hairnet, the old cook has a serious face. Her spotless white uniform seems to have ritual significance. The dance is cool, languid, almost stately in its dignity. At the same time, it is powerfully alive. It expresses unity, unity of movement, unity of purpose.

Denise prompts Margie through the changes with a big-sisterly grip of the hand. They lean to the right, kick, turn, cross their feet. Then clap! Denise lets go. And Margie claps too. With no prompting, Margie makes another turn, a squat, step forward, step backward, and a twist of the hips. Another clap. Now separated from Denise, Margie becomes connected to the line. The line has become a living thing, a joining of individual bodies into one dancing mass, a kind of joining that does not depend on touch. Dancing in her faded yellow church dress, Margie radiates competence beyond question. Where did she learn to dance like that?

I guess I'm gawking pretty bad because Sara's looking at me instead of the dancing, and looking at me like I'm a hick. "You never seen stepping? I guess you wouldn't have." Her eyes turn back to the dancing, and she's smiling, without irony, without reservation. "Now, that's the way it should be. Campers, counselors, and cooks. United." Then anger sparks. "Why do things get so screwed up?"

There is nothing I can say. The dancing line is beautiful, that's all.

The last note fades out, and there is a moment's hush before the line breaks up and they are again individual people, seven individual laughing people wrapped around the old cook in a chaotic embrace. When they release her, she too is laughing, bent low at the waist, hand over her mouth. Slapping her thighs, she steps backward all the way into the kitchen.

Arm in arm, Denise and Margie walk off the dance floor. Only when they have rejoined the white people does Margie change back. She stares at her feet. She is shy again.

"Last dance!" Mr. Bob calls.

Back at the cabin, there is talk of boyfriends.

"Last year at camp I really fell for this guy," Yvonne says. "He had mild CP. He used a three-footed walker, and he was always falling down, getting injured, breaking stuff. Such a slob. Now I can't remember why I thought he was so great, but I spent every minute I could with him. We found all kinds of places to sneak off and do things. I wrote to him, but he never wrote back."

"So you'll have to find somebody else. Somebody better!" Denise says.

"Yeah. That para is pretty good-looking."

"Him? The King of the Formerly Normal?"

"Hey, I'm formerly normal too, you know." Yvonne's laughing.

"I saw you two dancing and him talking and you giggling up a storm," Peggy Jo says. "But he thinks he's too cool!"

"So who do you like?" Yvonne asks.

"I've been seeing this guy at home. My sister's a cashier at the A&P, and he works there after school. My sister says I shouldn't tell guys I'm in special ed. She says when I'm out of school, she'll get me a job at the A&P and I'll live a normal life."

"I've tried that," Denise confesses. "But I don't know. Sooner or later they find out I'm epileptic. Epileptics can't get married. It's against the law." An awkward silence comes. Denise is embarrassed. She takes a light tone.

"And what about you, Miss Margie? I bet every young man in tobacco country is after you!"

"Naw. Not every one."

"But somebody? Who?"

"Just this one fellow is always looking at me in church."

"Well, well, and what are you doing when this fellow is looking at you?"

"Nothin'." Margie scrapes the floor with her foot.

"Nothin'?" Denise teases. "Not even looking back, maybe a little quick sideways look?"

Margie hides her whole face behind her hands. "Maybe!"

"Nothing wrong with that!"

I don't want to admit that I've never had a boyfriend, never been on a real date. I went to the junior-senior dance with a big crowd of friends and always had some guy to keep me company while the others danced, but there's never been one special guy for me. I know I'll meet someone someday—maybe in college—and get married. I might even meet someone here at camp. Maybe I'll get to talk to that surfer guy. I can almost feel his fingers wrapped around mine, moving in time to the music.

Sara has her nose in a book. "Hey, Sara," Yvonne says, "don't you have some words to share on this subject?"

"Well. I come from a long line of old maids. About half the women in my mother's family—and five of the seven Saras—were old maids. They were independent scholars. I think I'd be one of them even if I weren't crippled. I'd be happy in a convent, if they'd take atheists, but being crippled it makes that much more sense. In the marriage market, I'd be damaged goods. Better to stay off the auction block."

"You don't believe in God?" Yvonne is astonished.

The conversation moves on to religion. I want to tell Sara she's wrong about being an old maid. There's someone for everyone. She'll find someone to love, someone to love her. Maybe some strange guy like Abraham in the Bible. But nothing I say can make any difference. She has to figure everything out for herself.

*The circle is a perimeter. As such, it describes
an area and creates a division between within
and without, embraced and rejected,
included and excluded.*

"At least you let him keep the sports sec-tion."

"Yeah, just shows how nice I am, how generous, how giving!" Sara has talked Mr. Bob into giving her his morning paper. She spreads the *Charlotte Observer* across the picnic table in front of the lodge.

I look at the headlines and think about Mr. Bob, right now, inspecting our cabin. He crawls under our beds. No dust. No sand. He climbs up into the rafters. No cobwebs. He's more and more frustrated. Margie's hospital corners are perfect.

"Oh, great! Another letter to the editor about student protesters. Listen to this idiocy." She reads the letter in a crotchety old man's voice, stressing all the trite phrases. Silent majority. A loud-mouthed few. Spoiled. Permissive parents.

My face breaks into a grin, not because of the reading,

but because I'm thinking of Mr. Bob down at our cabin. He sees the blinds absolutely straight, all pulled to exactly the same height, with each cord coiled around a nail. That's another one of Margie's ideas; it will make him crazy. If Sara will just get going with our skit for Talent Night, we're sure to win the inter-cabin competition. If she'll just stop talking long enough, I'll ask her about it.

She takes the letter all the way to its crotchety conclusion. "Our generation knows what it's like to work for a living. It's time for them to find out." I laugh, but I also wonder if I would have found the article so stupid if I had been reading it myself. My dad often expresses similar views.

Over Sara's shoulder I look at the comics. "Sa-ra, when are you going to write the skit for Ta—"

I hear some sort of commotion down toward the lake. I can't make it out. It's a voice, possibly angry. Now, I hear it, clearly—a howl of rage.

"Noooooo," it bellows. "No. No. No. No." It gets louder. Now it's unmistakable: it's the aussie. Robert. We listen. I think I hear Norm calls of alarm, but they're just background noise, static, overpowered by the roar of Robert's rage.

Now the voice is making words. Human words. Words that strike the lake's smooth surface and resound in bell-like clarity over the whole camp:

"I AIN'T GONNA RIDE IN NO FUCKING CANOE!"

With a crackle, the newspaper page Sara was turning falls to our feet. Our heads turn toward the voice.

"Right on, Robert!" Sara yells loud enough to be heard all the way down there. At the same instant, I send forth a wordless animal sound, half squeal, half roar—most definitely a cheer.

Other voices join ours. From the boys' cabins overlooking the lake. From the dock. From the path up the hill to the lodge. On the way to the stable. Pandemonium. The chorus swells like ocean waves and merges with what's left of Robert's roar.

Sue rushes out of the lodge. "Be quiet, girls. We don't want to reinforce Robert's inappropriate language."

"Inappropriate?" Sara sputters. "Surely Robert's language is very appropriate. In fact, it's the only appropriate language I've heard from him in eight years."

"Don't be so smart."

"But isn't it great? He knows they're trying to put him in a canoe. He knows he doesn't want to get in. And he's figured out how to say it. Loud and clear."

"Yeah." My voice is squeaky. I'm flushed. Sue ignores me and looks at Sara with a face that says "there she goes again."

"He's like us," I say.

I know, five minutes ago I'd have been insulted if someone suggested I had something in common with Robert. Now I know better. He's dropped his mask, a mask he's worn for at least eight years. Maybe he'll wait another eight years before dropping it again, if he ever does. But this one time has been enough. Enough to know: he's like us.

I can't get the words out to explain all this, but no need. Sara knows. She understands my telegram-short speech, just as we both understand volumes from Robert's yell. Only the Norms don't get it.

The excitement subsides. In a transformation that is almost physical, the event is becoming a Camp Memory. I have no doubt Willie and Sara will turn it into a Camp Story. Their version will be funny and probably slightly mean, but I think it should be a different kind of story, a beautiful story of a precious revelation, a marvel. The problem is, I'm no good at telling stories. And anyway, who would listen? The people back home would never understand. You have to be here.

Maybe it's a mark of how few adventures I've had that getting here, to this little cottage, almost seemed like an adventure. It's only a pocket of pine woods in eastern North Carolina, but I imagined I was deep in some foreign Black Forest as we wound through clouds of sand gnats and buzzing mosquitoes and the possibility of unseen snakes. A tangle of trees trapped the air and blocked the sun, and we kept going with no view of where we were headed. At last we turned a bend, seemingly no different from all those other bends that got us nowhere, and there it appeared, the little cottage, sun-bleached, squatting on an egg-shaped yard of swept white sand, a reverse oasis of light, sand, and open air, ringed entirely by dense green wilderness. That first encounter promised fairy-tale magic. But here, now, inside, there's only Camp Courage reality. It's time for arts and crafts.

We take our places with some boys at paint-spattered tables under three naked lightbulbs that hang from the ceiling. We have been given heavy cardboard, pencils, and Elmer's glue. Silently I listen to the demonstration: how to make mosaics. The arts and crafts coordinator, Becky, is as cute and perky as the two little ponytails bouncing on either side of her head, but I tune her out. I also tune out the boys' joking and teasing. I'm too busy studying all the things on the table: piles and piles of dried beans, buttons, beads, and macaroni. I could try all day and never pick up even one thing. In occupational therapy, I tried very hard to sort screws and bolts that were bigger than these things, but I just couldn't get hold of them.

The lecture's over, and Sara asks me what I want my bean mosaic to be. "A tree," I tell her. What am I saying? I won't be making a mosaic.

"Any particular kind?"

"Twis-ty."

"Twisty? Right." She shakes her head, but goes ahead and pencils in an outline of a twisty tree. I nod agreement.

"Margie, I think this is your department now."

Good. Sara and Margie are evidently old hands at making bean mosaics. Margie squeezes glue on Sara's lines, and then carefully lays alternating rows of coffee beans and field peas, first up the length of the tree and then over the branches.

"Now, what about leaves?"

"But-ter beans."

The three of us hunch over the picture together. I watch and Sara directs and Margie sticks two or three butter beans at the end of each branch. It comes into being as a recognizable oak tree, a pleasing balance of irregular curves.

Perky Becky stands over us and ruffles my hair. "Hey, that's really beautiful." I smile; it is nice. But Sara designed it, and Margie did the work. They deserve the compliment. Becky knows that.

"You need to do one for yourselves," she tells Sara and Margie. "Time's almost up."

Sara holds the glue upside down and waits. When all the glue is below all the air in the bottle, a very slight squeeze produces an even flow of white goo. Freehand, she pours out a circle of glue. Then she segments the shape with three gluelines, one long, two short. It's a peace symbol, what my grandma calls the Devil's Footprint. Margie starts laying a single row of red beans on the top, and Sara attacks the bottom. In no time their arcs meet, closing the shape and making it complete.

I have showered off the sweat from arts and crafts and the algae from swimming and am back in our cabin sitting between the oscillating fans. My goal is to keep cool for a while. We aren't due at the lodge for almost two hours.

"Sara, when are we go-ing to start work-ing on our skit for Tal-ent Night?"

"It's under control. Don't worry about it."

I'm slightly annoyed, but no one else seems concerned. They're perfectly happy to sit around like old people on a front porch and spend the afternoon in pointless talk-ing. It happens at some point every day: there's nothing to do except to just be while the schedule catches up with itself.

Sara sticks stamps on two postcards. Then, with languid ease, just like my grandma dropping snapped beans into a colander and trash into a paper bag, she tosses the postcards on her cot. I think she wants me to notice them. One is addressed to her family in Charleston and the other to her mother in Madrid, Spain.

"My mom's leading a student tour," she explains casually.

I can hardly believe it. My mom might go to the beauty parlor on her own, but not if she can get someone to go with her. I'm curious now, and I take a peek at the books on Sara's bed. I don't know what to make of them. They are not romances, not thrillers, not titles from the high school reading list.

"Is this what they read in crip-pled school?"

"This is what *I* read in crippled school. Most people in my crippled school can't read; it's not exactly expected. These are from the library at my father's college."

I pick up the black book, *The Political Theory of Possessive Individualism*, and drop it in my lap. Sara launches in. "This is by a terrific Marxist historian, and he's explaining how we came to look at the world the way we do. Like, you know, the idea that politics should reflect the choices of individual people, that contracts define relationships, markets distribute goods, the state's job is to protect property. All that shit."

I turn the pages with my knuckles and try not to crunch the soft cream paper. On some pages, the footnotes take up more space than the text. It looks excruciatingly boring. "Why are you in-ter-es-ted in all that?"

She leans forward on her folded legs. "Mainly because I'm trying to figure out being crippled. Why are we the dregs? Why are we the outcasts? Because we deserve it? I don't think so. It's because of injustice. It's a failure of capitalism. Capitalism wants individualism, self-reliance, competition. If you can't compete, you starve. None of those things work for us."

I shouldn't encourage her, but I'm a little curious. "Are you say-ing we can ne-ver fit in?"

"Not truly. But in not fitting in, we're like the vast majority of people under capitalism. They don't fit in, but they don't know it. Marx talked about the alienating power of capitalism, which means most people become misfits, foreigners in their own countries. We try to fit in; we think we can fit in by imitating those who control things, but it's an illusion. False consciousness."

"Say what?" Denise teases. She's just walking in with Margie, fresh from the showers.

Sara won't be deflated. "Listen, it's real. We come to accept the views of our oppressors. We think there's something wrong with ourselves. It's like black people thinking they need to change the way they talk, lose their culture, get more white. They're fooling themselves. They need to ask why they can't be black AND equal."

"'You can't put a square peg in a round hole,'" Margie says. "You seen that on TV?"

"Yeah, Margie, you got it!"

Margie beams. Sara turns back to me. "It's an ad for Goodwill. The cripple is a sad square peg. Then rehab rounds off his corners and he's a happy face. But in the real world, our corners are permanent and incurable. If we could get over false consciousness, we might start changing the shape of the holes."

"Are you a com-mu-nist or what?"

"Communism's a beautiful dream. But it's not possible. I'm a socialist, and I think any sane cripple ought to be."

"I don't know a-bout that!"

She's so intelligent, but she knows nothing about the normal world. She doesn't go to normal school, and from what I can tell, her family isn't exactly normal either. From my own experience, I'm convinced that handicapped people can fit into the normal world. But I'm not going to argue the point.

I reach for the other book, slim and red. *Stigma: Notes on the Management of Spoiled Identity*, by Erving Goffman.

Again she doesn't wait to be asked. "I'm rereading that one. It's the best thing I've ever read about cripples. And homosexuals and prostitutes."

My eyebrow shoots up. "It's all one thing," she explains. "It's all about stigma. This book lays it all out— how stigma marks you as different, takes away the things that give people 'normal' identity. You're never just a girl, but always a crippled girl, a crippled student, a crippled daughter, a crippled sister. Your stigma determines what you can do.

"But what's so exciting about this book is that it describes how we *manage* our stigma. We take it and do something with it. We make choices."

"Like what?" Denise asks.

Sara shifts her weight from one elbow to the other and stretches her neck, warming up for the next lap. "Like, should we identify with our group or with the Norms? We can say, basically, to hell with the normal world and flaunt our differences like carnival freaks. Or we can accept Norm values."

"You mean like passing?" Denise asks.

"Kind of. The whole thing about stigma is that you can't ever be a Norm. So if you pass, it's only for a little while. The most you can really do is try to be *like* Norms. Or try to be what Norms want you to be. I think every cripple who can read should read this book." She glows enthusiasm like a revival preacher.

I think I might read this one someday, to see for myself what it's like. But I'm tired of being lectured at. "Sounds like you have eve-rything fi-gured out."

"Not quite, but I'm working on it."

Mr. Bob blows an earsplitting whistle. "Softball grand final! Everybody plays! It's the Greens against the Yellows." We divide into teams according to the color of the string on our name tags. Thus we avoid the awkwardness—the routine misery—of picking sides.

"There are no winners or losers," Mr. Bob says. "Everyone's a winner at Camp Courage!"

Each team has two girls' cabins and two boys' cabins. The game is organized so that, one way or the other, every camper gets a hit. The pitcher aims the ball right for the bat. Instead of "strike three," Mr. Bob calls "try again!"—sometimes six or seven times. Some campers find counselors' arms wrapped around them, holding the bat, and swinging. When all else fails, there are proxy arrangements.

It's my turn, and Carole pushes me up to the plate. "Do you think you can hold the bat?"

I reach out. Carole gently uncurls the fingers of my right hand and wraps them around the bat. I try to grip with my left hand too, but I can't get my two arms together.

"Let me help." A boy counselor I've never met has me locked up in his arms. "I've been looking for an excuse to get my arms around you." He smells like stale sweat.

"No, I got it." My voice is too loud, but I want to do it myself. The guy jumps out of the way before I spaz the bat right through his skull.

I raise the bat high in my right hand and swing experimentally, my arm extended almost straight from my shoulder. "Okay," I tell the pitcher.

The pitcher studies my crazy swing. Carefully he tosses a ball at my bat and almost hits it. He is good. Amazingly good. Our eyes meet, and we smile. This is like dancing; I'm moving with another person, trying to adapt my kind of movement to the kind of movement produced by natural grace. But I'm getting distracted from the job at hand. I need to make my bat whack the next ball that comes this way. That's all. I look away from the pitcher, toward the space the ball will cross, and nod that I'm ready. A ball comes, and I'm there a split-second too late. It's strike two, but nobody's counting. Another ball comes, and another miss. On the fourth try, the bat jumps loose. People scatter.

"We better get you some help, okay? You could've hit someone," Carole says.

I shake my head. "One more time. Just one." I wedge the bat against my left elbow and scrape it through my right fist until I have a tight grip near the center. My fingers burn, but I don't care. Give me one more chance. This time I'll hit that ball. I can feel it. I extend my arm. The bat's heavy, but my hold is solid.

I hold the bat high and let my spazzo energy surge through it. I'm wild and dangerous, brandishing this battle club. I don't see the ball, I'm too busy to look for it, but somehow I know it's coming, and I know it's fast, and without thinking I'm yelling, and I slam with all my strength. *Crack!* We've done it! The bat hits the ground like it's been shot down, and I thrust my wild dangerous right arm up to the sky and holler as my proxy runner, Sue, flies off.

It's a great moment, and I want it to last, but moments don't last, can't last, beyond a moment. Carole pushes me away from the plate, and the game moves on.

It's Sara's turn, and she doesn't want to play. She says something about "capitalism in microcosm."

"Please be a sport, Sara?" Carole says. "Please?"

She relents. "What the hell. Denise can proxy for me."

Denise runs up to confer with Sara. "Do you think he'll pitch high or low?"

"Softball is one thing I am completely ignorant of, okay? And I intend to remain ignorant. Just go on up. Do whatever you want. You're playing, not me."

Denise steps forward and makes a show of limbering up for the swing. From the sidelines, the crowd encourages her. "C'mon, Denise! Go!"

She takes her stance, waggling her hips in sweatpants.

"C'mon, Denise!" Willie yells, "Hit one for the GIMP!"

"Oh, please!" Sara laughs through a groan. He knows exactly how to get to her, how to get past whatever she's trying to do.

Denise is ready to swing. She gets her hit on the second pitch and easily makes it to second base. She is good enough to play softball for real.

At first I thought everyone would be allowed one home run, but now I see how it works. There are two separate games being played on one field, one for the proxies and one for the Crips. Proxies get no mercy from anyone. But Crips are allowed to move around the field without interference, except from other Crips. Crip fielding is so terrible that a camper on a walker makes it home; Yvonne, with her plastic leg and frazzled form, is one of the more valuable players.

Sue, out at third, made a big show of regret, coming

over and saying sorry. But when Denise makes it home, tying up the score for the Greens, people surround Sara with congratulations.

"Wait a minute," she objects. "I might be wrong, but I don't believe my big toe was out on that field. Could y'all please congratulate Denise?"

Why does she always have to be different? Why can't she play the game? I'm still flushed with the thrill of my big hit, the hit they didn't think I would get, and I wish she could share the excitment.

In this game where no one strikes out, an inning has to be redefined. An inning lasts until half the team has been at bat. The game is four innings long. In the end, the Yellow team—Willie's team—beats us. But we came close.

As darkness comes, we sports heroes walk, limp, shuffle, and are pushed in wheelchairs to a bonfire in a cleared space under trees nearby. An industrial-size bag of marsh-mallows stands by, waiting for the flames to rise. We gather in a circle. Illuminated by firelight, the inner ring of faces glows red and gold. The outer ring is more felt than seen, flashing into view only when the fire momen-tarily flickers bright. It is at once eerie and warm.

A girl counselor leads us in calm and soothing song: "Michael, Row the Boat Ashore," "I Gave My Love a Cherry."

Soon the sweet smell of marshmallows combines with the smell of pine smoke. Carole pops a marshmallow into my mouth. The toasty crust collapses under my teeth, and the hot, sweet goo slides down my throat. So good! I'm swallowing another when they start "Where Have All the Flowers Gone?" It's so sad, so sweet that the marshmallow sticks in my throat a little. "If I Had a Hammer" comes just in time to lift my spirits.

"Hey, Willie," I hear Sara say, "looks like the hippies of '68 are gone but not completely forgotten."

"Yeah, but I bet we won't be singing 'We Shall Overcome' this year."

"Or the political verses of 'This Little Light of Mine.'"

I leave them to their shared memories and political analysis and join the singing. Back home, I never sing. If asked, I'd say I can't sing, and that would be the truth: I can't carry a tune, or pronounce the words clearly, or get them out on the beat. But at Camp Courage it doesn't much matter. "Tell me why," I sing, "the ivy twines. . . ." I know all the words from hearing them year after year at church picnics, but this is the first time I've heard them coming from me.

The fire takes in a heavy branch. Fed by boiling sap, it flares, rumbling bright. Then there's a violent crack and the wood explodes. A slender stick breaks clear and is blasted, still burning, onto the clean sand. I watch it glow red, go black, then fade white as the smoke leaves. The fiber is consumed, and all that remains is a delicate curl of ash. I wonder how long it will keep its shape.

Staring at the ash, I listen. In my mind's eye, the word *cacophony* jumps out at me, right off the remembered page of some vocabulary workbook. But that word isn't adequate for what I hear. What I hear is more of an amalgamation, a stew of varied voices.

The counselor leads with a strong, clear voice. "Be-cause God ma-ade the i-vy twine." Among the other singers, campers and counselors, I hear scattered sweet harmonies. There is one good bass and a reasonable complement of sopranos, altos, and tenors. Somewhere in the mix, a marvelous Broadway baritone and a Motown falsetto. These voices will give us some competition on Talent Night, whatever we do. But mingled with the glee-club sounds are the hollow voices of MRs and maybe a deaf person. Slightly nasal tones and soft consonants—the mildest CP accent—unite with the many varieties of spastic singing. Some lack tune and rhythm; others follow a tune and rhythm of their own. There's a genuine bluegrass mountain twang. I hear the same voices that joined in cheering Robert this morning, but now their joining is patterned and structured. If it isn't always music, it is song, or at least the common pursuit of song. For all its oddness, it is singing.

I'm glad no one from Crosstown High is here. They wouldn't know what to make of these strange sounds.

But since no one else is here, I'm free to listen and to sing along.

"Because God made you, that's why I-I-I-I love you."

The singing ends. I look for that coil of white ash, but I can no longer make it out. It has lost its separate shape and merged with the sand.

To identify an object, it is necessary to refer to the group of which the object is a member or the whole of which it is a part. It is also necessary to specify the characteristics, qualities, or actions that distinguish the object from similar things.

"I won't be riding in a canoe," Sara says politely as soon as they park us on the dock.

The guy in charge shrugs. "Hey, no problem." It's that good-looking surfer type who really knows how to shag. I smile at him and watch his long brown legs carry him into the canoe. He is dazzling in the bright light of mid-morning.

"Robert's rebellion has hegemony walking on eggs," Sara whispers.

"I can take two at a time on the canoe," the surfer guy says. "While y'all wait, Bobby can show you how to fish."

I already know how to fish. Dad likes to say it's an essential part of a girl's education. Bobby, a brawny boy in a baseball cap, gives us bamboo fishing poles baited with plastic worms. "Now, you have to keep real quiet, or you'll scare the fish away!" He speaks to us like we're children.

Peggy Jo steps carefully into the canoe. Mary follows, fearless, like a sleepwalker.

"Aw, too bad," Sara says. "I was hoping the aussies had somehow organized a general strike of all activities. But Mary's not resisting."

Mosquitoes hum around us, but no one moves. On the water the cork floats are just as inert. Nothing is happening. Nothing is likely to happen, either. No self-respecting fish will bite a bright green hard plastic worm. That much is obvious. Not that lures and bait can't be a matter of debate; Dad and his fishing buddies can argue for hours about what to use where. However, in a sandy-bottomed black-water lake, pond really, live earthworms are what you need.

The canoe has glided away. I try to make out the surfer guy's voice, but all I can hear is the sound of Sara's pastels scratching across the rough paper.

Sara's drawing is becoming a picture of this place. The foreground is still in outline: cattails, the strip of sand, a spindly pine branch arching upward. On the horizon, a hill and tall pines beyond the lake. The shapes are right, but trees should be green; these are a jumble of blues, browns, and purples, with spots of orange and red. What green there is, is incidental. And then the lake—that cool, dull black sheet I love to wrap up in—is being rendered as a warfare of color: blues fighting reds, oranges against greens, blues versus grays. Here, one side dominates, there another. In some places, there's such a melee that you can't tell who's winning.

Sara squints, so I squint too. Now I see; I can imagine the final effect. Unable to take in so many jarring extremes, the eye tricks itself into seeing a tame and muted scene.

It is this place, and not this place. There is no dock. No safety-orange floating barrels. No man-made body parts on the shore. No sign that it was all built by the Jaycees, with invaluable help from the Honorable State Senator B. J. McNeill. It's a typical North Carolina fishing hole, just like a normal lake.

Our corks hang lifeless in the water. Well, I can always hope. There are supposed to be lots of fish down there. If I catch one, maybe that dancing cook will fry it for me. Or maybe not. Probably, they'd make me let it go.

Now the corks are bobbing but not because fish are biting; the canoe is coming back. The sounds come near. Lapping paddles, the pleasant voice of the surfer guy. I look up to smile at him and only then realize how tense I am.

Even with help, I won't be able to step into the canoe. They'll have to lift me. I hate being lifted. The thought of being hauled into a little wobbly boat fills me with dread. But really I don't have much choice. I have to trust these guys. They must know what they're doing; they've been doing it all summer. It will be fine.

"Who's next?" With the sun behind him, the surfer

guy's body makes a lean silhouette and his hair shines silver. Around him, light bounces off the black water like flashbulbs.

"Me?" I say. Might as well.

The other guy wrestles me into a life vest and takes hold of my shoulders. Kneeling in the canoe, the surfer grips me tight around my knees.

"Got her?" Bobby asks.

"Yeah," he answers.

"One, two, three," they yell. "Up!"

With one yank I'm out of my chair. My disconnected body spans the dock and the boat. The little boat lurches to the side, strains against the rope, is near to overturning.

"Whoa!" the surfer guy hollers. With one arm he's reaching for the dock while the other takes harder hold of my legs. The other guy has me hanging by my shoulders.

I can't see where I've been or where I'm going. There is no up, no down, no left, no right. My body wants escape. My back stiffens, and I nearly throw the guy off my shoulders. At the same time, a furious leg kicks the surfer guy hard in the chest.

"Christ! For Christ's sake, be still!" He sounds angry. He tightens his hold and slams my knees together with such force I wonder if they'll crack.

"Stop! Hold it!" The other guy is straining against me. I'm making it harder, even dangerous. My mind tells my body to submit, don't fight. But my body won't give in.

"Hang on! Got her?"

"Got her!" I try to stop fighting, but just as hard I try to escape. I try to escape, but I'm caught. I can't move. My strength is no match for the combined strength of two able-bodied men determined to subdue me.

"Over now!"

"Okay!"

"Down!" The surfer guy drops my legs, and I think my shoulder joints may come apart with the weight of my body. My spine grazes the dock's wooden lip; my feet hit the rocking boat; my tailbone bangs onto a plank seat. The guys turn loose. I lie there, too exhausted to try to sit up. I feel the surfer guy right beside me, breathing hard.

As soon as I can speak, I say I'm sorry. I didn't mean to knock the wind out of him.

He doesn't hear. He's up again, giving Margie a hand down.

Gingerly, Margie sits down beside me. "Hey, you okay?" I feel her warm hand push my hair back from my brow; it's one of those sweet comforting gestures that make you want to cry. Sprawled in the canoe, I close my eyes. I make myself feel the sun bake my face and listen to the water lapping underneath. With all my will, I rein in my limbs. I can't force myself to relax, but I reestablish the tension and countertension that will stop the crazy movements and let me look calm. I open my eyes to the cloudless sky, bend my knees, pull up my back, and sit up. I note the position of the shore. I am ready to go.

The canoe glides across the lake. The surfer explains how the Indians made canoes with burned-out tree trunks. I try to be interested. I try at least to act interested. If I try hard enough, maybe I can enjoy the ride.

However, even my special knack for contentment can't quite carry me. I dread the lift out of the canoe. I don't want that cute guy to wrestle me like a wild animal. I don't want to kick him again.

Maybe I should have refused to get in this effing canoe. I censor the bad word in my thoughts.

Maybe. But too late now.

Maybe getting out won't be so bad. I'll be handed up to a solid place. That will be much better.

But they'll have to catch me first.

My mind turns on the best way to get back in my chair. They can roll me out of the canoe into the lake; I'll float back to the shallow water and they'll walk me to my chair on the shore, just as they do every day after swimming. But this is a silly idea. A shower and change aren't in the schedule.

The surfer guy demonstrates paddling techniques and hands the paddle to Margie. Margie plies the paddle from side to side with real grace, but every so often she steals a sideways look at me. I flash a big grin at her and then at the surfer guy. I want to say everything is fine, but I don't speak. Something like fear, something like shame, holds me back.

We turn back to the dock. There is the weathered ladder-backed chair that serves as Sara's easel, and beside it is the empty wheelchair. My chair. My comfortable place, loyally waiting for my return.

We get nearer, and I see that the dock is barely two feet higher than the plank I'm sitting on. The drop seemed so huge! Now I know what to do. The surfer guy will keep the boat steady. He won't need to touch me. The other guy will sit on the dock. I'll turn my back to him and push up with my feet; he'll pull just enough to set my rear-end on the dock. I'll be on something solid. Getting in the chair will be fairly difficult, but I know how. Pulling on a borrowed arm, I'll get on my knees, then pull out one leg. Pressing that foot hard against the boards, I'll rise up. Then plop! into my chair.

I visualize the process in the moment it takes them to tie up the canoe. But explaining it to these guys—if I could do it at all—would take a lot of words and a very long time. Easier to let them handle me the way they've handled every other spazzo all summer long. In just a few seconds it will be over.

After lunch, I stretch out on my cot. I've made it out of the canoe in reasonably good shape, but the ordeal still affects me. My body aches.

I watch Carole lift Sara onto her cot. Carole is petite and delicate-looking, the kind of girl guys carry stuff for, but in fact she's strong. Of course, Sara is really tiny, a wraith. The easy pliability of her body always surprises me. When she's up in her chair, talking, organizing things, she's an unyielding personality, a person entirely separate and distinct. In Carole's arms, those qualities melt away; she looks snug, even cuddly. Seeing her body mold itself to Carole's hollows arouses not only my curiosity but also something like envy.

If I were floppy and soft like her, I'd be happy for that surfer guy to lift me up and carry me around in his arms. I'd curl up in his lap, fill his hollows, and let him paddle our canoe across the lake and deep into the woods on twisty black-water creeks. And we'd eat all the fish we'd catch.

Now Sara sits cross-legged on her cot, cuddly no longer, writing on typing paper. She fills a whole page with writing and slips another sheet out of the plastic package. Around then, heat and exhaustion and the relentless rhythm of the oscillating fans finally overcome my nerves. I join the others in sleep.

I am restless in arts and crafts. This isn't my thing to begin with, and it's a kind of torture to sit here with paint fumes hanging in the air. Getting back to the cabin is like being freed from jail.

Sara is going through her papers. "What is all that?" I ask.

"I was busy while y'all were napping." She turns to address the whole room. "You know, the scuttlebutt is that we're way ahead on Cabin Cleanup; the Yellows won softball, but Margie and Denise have racked up some points for us in sports. We're clearly ahead overall. On Talent Night, we'll cinch Best Cabin All Around. I have here the winning skit."

"Oh, yeah?" Although I'm teasing her a little, I'm more than ready to forget about what happened this morning and hear about the skit.

"It's called 'Morning at Camp Courage.' Y'all get the idea? Denise and Peggy Jo can play the counselors."

"I've got to have your T-shirt, Sue," Denise says, "and that whistle!"

"You were going to be Carole, but if you want to be Sue, that could work." She flips through the script and jots notes.

Peggy Jo gets a dreamy look in her eyes and wrestles with a hunk of hair. "I can be Carole, if y'all want me to, not that I have to, or anything."

"I'm not that bad, y'all. Am I?" Carole says. I've never noticed her soft country accent, but Peggy Jo has captured it just right.

Sara gets down to business. "Basically, the situation is, heroic counselors struggle through the morning routine and have a series of humorous encounters with sleepy-heads, grumps, layabouts, and bubble-brains."

"Can I be a layabout?" Margie asks.

"A layabout? You? I was thinking more like a would-be cosmetologist. You'll be doing Jean's hair and makeup. Does anyone know how to build one of those awful beehives?"

My aunt has one of those beehives. It would take a whole can of hairspray to get my fine hair to do that, but it could be funny.

"What about Dolly? What will she be doing, do you think?" Carole asks.

"She'll be herself, talking about her novella."

Carole looks at Sue with an unspoken question on her face. Sue frowns but doesn't say anything.

"And Yvonne will be forging fraudulent BM charts. We need a good joke about BM charts. Or about forgery. I haven't got it yet." I squeal at the idea. Pretty risqué, Dolly would say.

"And, Sara," Denise asks, "exactly what will you be doing all this time?"

"I'll be trying to convince everyone to strike. I'll give a Marxist analysis of cabin cleanup as a form of labor exploitation. My rousing oratory will be unheeded because of your false consciousness, of course."

I laugh. Isaac. We laugh. Even at our own favorite theories.

"What a-bout Ma-ry?" I ask.

"She'll be the very best. You know how aussies copy-cat. We'll put her off to the side, with a big roll of toilet paper. Someone will have to get her started, but all the way through the skit she'll be breaking off the squares, one by one, saying 'He loves me, he loves me not.' Before long there'll be this big pile of toilet paper squares on the floor, and the counselors' brooms will send them flying. It'll get funnier and funnier."

"I don't know," Carole says. "Don't you think maybe—"

"Carole's absolutely right," Sue says. "It's not appropriate to make fun of Mary and encourage her autistic tendencies. I think you'll need to change Dolly's part too."

"Okay then," Sara challenges them. "You think up something, something appropriate, for both of them, for all of us if you don't like this skit. But I tell you, this skit will be funny. And it will score the points we need. Remember Commissar Bob's Rule Number One!"

"Everyone participates!" we yell.

We're sure to have the best skit. My competitive blood is up, and the first rehearsal is underway.

"What do you want to do?" Sara asks. For the evening, the lodge has been transformed into a carnival crowded with booths.

I shrug.

"Well, if you don't have any special preferences, I have

an idea. Let's just reconnoiter for a while and agree to play the first game somebody loses."

I'm puzzled but nod agreement. Whatever.

Margie walks between Sara and me and pulls us by our armrests through the crowd. Without getting in line to play, we get close enough to see the action at the first booth. The front of the booth is a cross-section of the sea on brown paper. Behind the blue waves are big steel basins from the kitchen. In the basins float yellow plastic fish, each with a ring on its back. The objective is to hook a fish with a weighted fishing hook.

There is no limit on how many times a camper can try. When necessary, the counselor grabs the fish and holds it still. Dead on the water. The camper swings the hook. Nowhere near. The counselor tries holding the line a few inches from the hook and dangles it toward the ring. "This is really pretty hard," she says. To get it over with, she holds the fish and hooks it. All the camper has to do is bring it in. The plastic fish doesn't put up much of a struggle.

"Not exactly *The Old Man and the Sea* is it?" Sara says.

Willie comes up from behind and leans on my push handles. "What are y'all doing?"

Margie answers. "Reconnoitering. What about you?"

"I'm on a mission. The guys in my cabin sent me to find out what y'all are doing for Talent Night."

"Oh, really?" Sara says.

"When we were outside waiting, we split up, you know,

and stealthily eavesdropped on everyone. We caught them rehearsing, right out in the open. Now we know our competition. Except you guys. Y'all weren't rehearsing."

"We don't need to re-hearse!" I squeal.

"We're good," Margie says.

"And we don't want you stealing our material," Sara adds. "So go back to your cabin, Double-O-Seven, and tell the guys your slick and subtle espionage came up dry!"

"At least I tried."

Through my push handles I feel him leave.

At the next table a girl counselor in a slinky dress is running a blackjack game. The para gets beaten by the bank. Yvonne is standing there watching, playing the high roller's floozy.

"Okay," the croupier declares, "that hand was for practice. Now the real deal."

The para looks at his cards. "Hit me," he says.

She shows him the next card, an eight. "Might be risky."

"Okay, then don't." He gives Yvonne the plastic love beads he wins. She gives him a little kiss, and her beige skin goes red.

The next camper can't add to twenty-one. The hints get even more direct. Each player is a winner, and each winner gets a hug from the croupier.

In the basketball game, the hoop moves to suit the thrower's ability. When the quad plays, Sue holds the ball up to his chin, and the basket touches his knees. He gives the ball a tap, and it falls on his lap and rolls straight into the basket. Another sports hero.

The Gypsy fortune-teller predicts happiness, wealth, luck, and love for all. There are no struggles, no setbacks, no perils in her crystal ball.

"You will have good health and long life," we hear her tell Robert the aussie behind her curtain.

"Oh, yeah," Sara scoffs. "So that's why they're lining up to sell him insurance!"

"Gotta go to Gozeboro . . ."

We hear Willie's laugh explode behind our backs. "Willie," Sara says, "you've blown your cover. We knew you were lurking around anyway. Just forget about getting any intelligence from us!"

"You said it, I didn't."

The games start looking pretty similar. There are a circus game, a rodeo game, a safari game, all with the object of throwing something and knocking something down. I kind of want to try. Once I get hold of a ball, I can throw a good distance, with a lot of force. My aim is erratic, but I like a challenge. We spazzos are pretty good at knocking things down.

I watch the games. Everyone is winning. Most of the prizes are little things. Penny candies, bubblegum, plastic jewelry, rubber bugs. However, there are some real prizes: stuffed animals, hats, T-shirts.

We keep moving.

Margie says, "Seems like everyone's got one good prize. Except us." She's right. I wonder if she wants a prize. We head to the circus game.

Sue comes over. "Are y'all playing?"

"Not yet," Sara says.

"Well, what are you waiting for?"

"We've decided to play the first game someone loses, because we'll know that game isn't rigged."

Mr. Bob overhears. "Hey, now, everyone is a winner at Camp Courage!" He gives Sue an obvious wink. "What makes you think the games are rigged?"

Sara makes an exaggerated show of patience, "Oh, it's hard to say. I just have a nagging feeling. Maybe it's completely unjustified, so I promise I'll play as soon as someone proves me wrong by losing."

"Sara," Sue says, "I'm tired of your inappropriate behavior. It's bad enough when you continually refuse to participate, but now you're spoiling the fun for others. I want you to stop this. Right now."

"Sue, the 'others' can do whatever they want. But I'm not playing until someone loses. I'm just watching. I'm not making a scene. Now, if you want a scene, by all means, carry on."

Mr. Bob leans down to talk to Margie, which is unnecessary because she's nearly as tall as he is. "Wouldn't you like to play?" he asks. "I bet you'd like to win a prize."

Margie grins stupidly at her sneakers. "No thanks, Mr. Bob. I likes to pull the wheelchairs around. It's fun."

"Jean, what about you?"

"Not now."

Mr. Bob turns away for a quiet discussion with Sue. It is quickly concluded. "I can't force you to play," Sue tells Sara, "but be sure you don't interfere with anyone else." It sounds like a threat, but from the way she and Mr. Bob hurry away, it's clear they're surrendering.

Dolly is at the circus game, howling and drooling. Her proxy, that marvelous softball pitcher, easily topples a clown. We go on to the safari game. A guy is very close to the lion—close enough to touch it, if he only had sense enough to reach out—but he can't manage to bag it. "Try again," they tell him. Someone shakes the table until the lion falls down.

It's that surfer guy, shaking the table. I want to vanish; I don't want him to notice me and remember how hard I kicked him. Why doesn't Margie pull us away? We stay right there, right in front of the surfer guy. Since I can't vanish, I look right at him. I brave a smile. I say, "Hel-lo."

"Hello," he says. I see no sign of recognition. Then it occurs to me: This morning, as he grappled with me, as he squeezed my legs hard enough to hurt, as I kicked him, he never looked at my face. Maybe he doesn't know me from any other wheelchair girl in this place.

We move from one knock-down game to another. No

one ever loses, and therefore we can't play. No matter. I've lost the desire.

Back in the cabin, Dolly brags about how she won a huge purple teddy bear. Sara and I say nothing. We don't intend to spoil anyone's fun. It seems that everyone had a good time. Maybe they didn't notice that the games were rigged, or didn't care. They all feel like winners.

When the games are rigged, does it make everyone a winner—or no one? All I know is that I don't feel much like a winner. But I don't feel like a loser either. That's something. It is better that I didn't get with the program this time. I believe in competition. The program seems to say that handicapped people aren't up to it; we can only pretend to be winners. I don't want to pretend. I want to achieve, really achieve. Or I will take my disappointments just like anyone else.

Day Seven

Equilibrium is the apparent stasis that results from a dynamic process, the product of forces acting with equal strength in opposite directions.

Soon camp will be over, and my camera hasn't moved from the ledge where I dropped it that first day. On my way out, I grab it. The screen door slaps behind me, and my casters thud across the gangway.

Outside, Margie is taking towels off the clothesline.

I hold up my camera. "Carole," I say and nod toward Margie.

Carole looks through the viewfinder, ready to snap.

"Wait." I see the photo in my mind. It's dark shade, but if I'm lucky, it will be good. Gentle light on Margie's dark chocolate face. Focus sharp on the nap of the blue towels. In the background, a blur of green and brown vegetation. "Set that lit-tle button, yep, on three. Now move to the left. Not so much. Get the yel-low tow-el in the mid-dle." My voice gets high and squeaky. "Mar-gie, smile."

Margie bends her head toward the clothespin she cradles in her hand and then glances up with her shy smile. The shutter clicks. I can see how the photo will look in my album. When my folks flip to that page, they'll probably ask, "What's wrong with the colored girl?" I'll have to tell them Margie is mentally retarded. Mildly. For a second, I wish, for Margie's sake, that I hadn't taken the picture. But then, my folks ought to know about her. How nice she is. How helpful. I can make them understand. I think I'll use up the whole roll of film.

Sara rattles over the planks just behind me. "You make me think of my grandmother!" We roll toward the lake. "She can't cook—not even rice—but she can sure tell other people what to do. She calls it 'executive ability.' You've got it too!"

It's true. I don't need to hold the camera; I can explain what to do. Maybe it's odd, but what else am I supposed to do?

At the lake, I get a good shot of Sue and Carole together on the dock. I get Peggy Jo strapping a life vest on Mary and Yvonne making rabbit ears over Denise's swimming-cap-covered head. I want a picture of Sara working on her drawing.

"Sorry," Sue says, "Sara's picture can't be taken."

"Oh, yeah, doc-tor's or-der." I raise my eyebrow at Sara, and she smirks back at me. I leave my camera with her and stomp cheerfully into the lake.

"Did you take the photos in your scrapbook?" Sara asks. "I mean, other than all those telethon glamor shots."

"Most of them." I open my mouth to beef stew. Camp Courage stew.

"You know, things really are upside down in this world."

I raise an eyebrow.

"The more severely disabled you are, the crappier job you get, if you get a job at all. Like, maybe, stuffing envelopes, on a piece-rate."

Peggy Jo joins the conversation. "A wheelchair girl who used to go to my school got a job at a workshop drawing big Xs on cardboard cones from a textile mill."

"Oh, God, what a life!" With glassy eyes, Sara pantomimes picking up cones and drawing Xs. Then her eyes get sharp again. "Why did they want Xs on the cones?"

"I don't know. She never said. She was just glad to have a job."

"You see, Norms give us drudge work and call it rehabilitation, never mind if we have executive ability. No telling what we could do if we had two or three Norms to boss!"

I don't see myself having two or three Norms to boss— or putting Xs on cones. I'll go to college and maybe get into computers. I've never seen a computer, but I think I could be a programmer. I'm good with details, and I can type, very slowly but accurately. I don't know, but I do know that I won't wind up in some workshop. Maybe that's what the kids at Butner and in crippled schools do, but I'm one of the top students at Crosstown High. Our top students go to college.

I suck some iced tea through a straw. "I plan to go to col-lege to get a job using my brain. In com-pu-ters."

"Where? Chapel Hill? They've got Norms fighting each other to get in. They don't take Crips. Even if your mother or sister went along to take care of you, they don't take Crips."

"I got into Cross-town High, and they did-n't take han-di-capped peo-ple ei-ther. Un-til me."

"Okay. Maybe. I mean, I hope you're right. My mother went to Chapel Hill; she makes it sound like paradise, so it would be great for you to be the first Crip at Chapel Hill." She sounds conciliatory but not convinced. She picks at the dry white rice that rings the stew. "If they have any sense, they'll take you and educate you to be a politician or head of a company or an army general—to use your executive ability!"

"What a-bout you? Next year you'll be in Norm-al school. You should try to get into col-lege."

"Actually, I probably will, if I live through high school. My mother's college just built a new campus with ramps and stuff. They told her they'll take me, since she'll be right there. Plus, they know I'm a card-carrying genius."

I ignore that. "What will you stu-dy?"

She digs under the stew to excavate a trench of rice. "History, economics, all that. You know, I want to figure everything out."

"And be a pro-fessor, like your pa-rents."

"I don't think so. They don't give Crips jobs that other people want. But I won't go to a workshop, and I won't be one of those inspirational crippled artists or writers. So I'll probably drag out school as long as I can, then maybe tutor something at home. But mostly I'll spend my last years as an ornament to society. Luckily, my family can give me a comfortable life. Odds are, I won't live long enough to go into a nursing home."

I am jolted.

"It's no big deal. Life's a terminal illness, with onset at birth. Everyone's terminally ill." Her flip delivery seems to cover something serious. "I just have a clearer idea of how it'll be. One winter I'll get pneumonia and the antibi-otics won't work. That's what happens to 'Jerry's kids,' you know. Don't you watch the muscular dystrophy telethon? You CP types do check out the competition, right?"

I do watch it, actually, but I can't connect her with those kids Jerry Lewis is trying to cure. 'Jerry's kids' are so tragic and sad. She's such a character. If Jerry offers her a cure, she might just turn him down flat! I don't know what to say. I wait for her to fill the silence with one of her lectures, but it doesn't come. I watch her untouched stew go cold. A shiny film forms on the top.

Finally, I say the only thing that comes into my head. "Jerry Lew-is does-n't know what he's tal-king about."

"Damn right!" I've made her laugh.

She turns her head. "Hey, Margie, you know why they call it Camp Courage stew?"

"Naw."

"It takes courage to eat it!"

"Courage you ain't got!"

"Courage I ain't got."

I would gladly eat her stew as well as my own. It isn't great, but if you stir it up, it's not bad. I'm still hungry.

They've pulled a movie screen over the big stone fireplace at the lodge. It's nearly time to see the movie the Soviet selected. For once, Sara's excited about an activity.

"You'll love it. There's this bit where Groucho dictates a letter to his lawyer, 'Hungerdunger Hungerdunger Hungerdunger Hungerdunger Hungerdunger & McCormick. Gentlemen. Question mark.' No wait, I think that's in *Animal Crackers*. In this one, Groucho sings 'Whatever it is, I'm against it.' Or that might be *Duck Soup*. It doesn't matter. I know Groucho does *something* really funny in this one. He always does!"

Mr. Bob stands up in front of the screen, but Sara is

still talking. "Margie, you've never seen the Marx Brothers? Harpo will just absolutely kill you!"

Mr. Bob speaks in his kindergarten way. "Tonight, we're going to enjoy a Disney Classic—"

"What did you say?"

Each of Sara's words pops out like a tiny explosion, but Mr. Bob pretends not to hear. "—it's called *Pollyanna*."

"What happened to *Horse Feathers*?" Sara insists. "The Soviet chose *Horse Feathers*."

Willie presses down on her back with both hands, almost like he's expecting her to jump out of her wheelchair by some miracle and attack someone. From the row in front of us, Carole turns back. "Listen, if you don't want to watch this? I can sit outside with you, okay?" She steps over her chair and pushes Sara toward the door.

Willie gets behind me and unlocks my brakes, and we follow Carole and Sara to the picnic table outside. Mr. Bob pretends to ignore Sara and talks, while Sara truly does ignore him and talks, talks with that kind of out-of-control control I've never seen in anyone but her.

"This place is completely beyond hope. The fucking arrogance of this place. To create a 'Camper Council,' and give it one trifling little task, to select one movie, one night, and then, without discussion, without reason, without even informing us, to take away that one trifling little choice, because maybe if we start making choices—even one trifling little choice—we'll get the idea that we're human beings instead of passive little freaks without a fucking brain in our heads . . ."

Her language makes me flinch, but Carole and Willie don't flinch. It seems that their job—our job—is to listen. I can't bear to listen, so instead I watch Carole listen. I see her patience, her growing sadness, as she listens until her wild hair goes limp. There's nothing to do but wait it out, until finally Sara falls silent. When she speaks again, the fury is spent, the irony returned.

"What can you do in a place like this? I guess *Horse Feathers* is inconsistent with the camp philosophy. It's unbridled silliness, way below zero on the inspirational scale. Obviously, inappropriate for us. What's appropriate is to spend our time in a strange mimicry of 'normal experiences'—dancing, playing softball, living the outdoor life. . . . But, of course, we don't really do these things, most of us; we just pretend to. The things we could really, truly enjoy together, freely, of our own choice, are counted worthless. To enjoy our day-to-day lives in our own way is forbidden." Again she pauses.

"What can you do in a place like this?"

"I'm so sorry," Carole says. She really is. "I think the way they handled it was wrong. They should have respected your choice. I'd rather see *Horse Feathers* myself, you know? But you have to forgive them because they don't understand. And you have to understand, that you—you three, I mean—are different from most of the campers in there. Most of them will like *Pollyanna*. Don't you think?"

"Well, maybe. But only because they've been brainwashed. They'd have liked *Horse Feathers* too, and maybe if we cut the inspirational crap, they'd find a way to be who they are. I just can't stand it. It's an insult to all of us, to who we are, and who we might become."

"Come on, Sara," Willie says gently, "you and I have been coming here a long time. We know it's nuts. It's always been nuts. It'll always be nuts. We can't expect it to get sensible. It's a camp for Freaks; we know the Norms that run it don't have the ghost of an idea what they're doing. But they don't matter. The Freaks are what matter. You know that. We share something here. Even though it's nuts, it's ours. Am I making any sense?"

Willie flashes his ghastly grin, and when she looks back at him, I remember her telling me that to her he is almost beautiful. I recognize an understanding between them that doesn't include me. I didn't grow up part of this place, or anyplace like this.

"I don't know," she answers. "I was hoping something would change. But this place is beyond repair. Maybe the best thing would be to pull it down."

As we've been sitting here together our shadows have lengthened and the sky has gone red. A small breeze stirs, and we take it into our lungs. The movie soundtrack comes through the screened walls and mingles with the sounds of night coming. Tree frogs. Crickets.

It is night when Carole speaks again. "Willie, you're definitely right about one thing. We don't have a clue. I came here with no idea what I'd be getting into. I had a vague idea that I wanted to serve. And I like it, when I'm really serving."

We keep silent to let her go on. "Am I crazy? I'm okay when I'm doing the physical work. Giving someone a shower, brushing hair, wiping someone's butt, even. I'm doing something that needs to be done. There's nothing complicated or awkward about it. But the idea of being a 'counselor' just seems ridiculous, you know? Y'all know, and I know, that I don't have a clue."

Willie's warm voice passes through the darkness. "Listen, if you come to Camp Courage and learn that you don't know what you're doing, you're miles ahead of most people going into the helping professions. Doesn't helping begin with admitting you don't know what to do? Most professionals storm in with all the answers. They see us as something to boss, not something to help."

Sara rests her chin on her fist, her eyes hidden in deep shadow. "But why must we be either thing? Something to help, or something to boss. Why can't we be people who do things, not always things people do unto? What would happen if we could find our power?"

Our talk stops there. The movie is ending, and inside

the screens the bright lights come on. Campers are moving past us on their way to the cabins. They have indeed enjoyed *Pollyanna*. I listen, finding myself hoping—hoping to hear someone, anyone—grouse about being shown a kids' movie. But all I hear is the usual racket of the campers on the move. Head 'em out! Move 'em in!

By now, the nightly drill is easy. I undress in the cabin. Sue covers me with a beach towel and runs me across the path. First the toilet. Then the sink. I open my mouth to my toothbrush. Sue brushes and holds a cup of water with a straw. I take in some water and spit it out. She rinses the toothbrush, brushes away the larger chunks of toothpaste, and takes a paper towel to my chin and neck. Next, to the shower.

"Sue!" Peggy Jo is screaming from outside. "Come quick! It's Denise! A seizure!" She bolts out the door, and I am left in front of the row of showers.

I look down and study the stripes on the beach towel on my lap. Then I look around me. During the time we've been here, inhibitions have been relaxed. For the first couple of nights, the counselors gave showers fully dressed. Now most are stripped down to their underwear and some are naked. All of the campers are completely exposed.

They are a strange assortment of bodies. I've become accustomed to them in their summer clothes, even in bathing suits. But seeing them naked is something else.

There is Yvonne. Every morning she puts a clean sock on her stump and straps on her leg and becomes one of the crowd. No one notices the plastic leg sticking out of her shorts. But here, attached to a naked body, otherwise normal, even beautiful, the oddness of it sticks out. Standing in the shower, she unhooks the leather harness and tosses the leg aside. She peels the white sock off her stump. Balancing on a grab bar, she stands there, naked, one-legged, and starts the shower. Sitting on a shower bench, stump jutting outward, she soaps herself and rinses and squeezes shampoo into the palm of her hand. She rubs shampoo into her hair, just like a two-legged girl with no thought of a stump. And why not? She is a one-legged girl, that's all. She must be used to it.

There are other shapes. Here is an interesting back, with a big fleshy bulge. Dangling from the body are tiny legs, frozen in their infant state. On another bench is a camper with a severe spinal curvature. Her back is so twisted that she sits on her side. Her breasts rest on her lap like two pillows on a mattress.

I stop seeing people and see body parts. Knees that look enormous because the shin muscles are gone. Skinny, useless limbs. Humps, bumps, and knots. Bags, tape, and gauze. Stomachs with holes in them and plastic tubes through which urine and feces escape. And more places where parts are missing.

At the far end of the room a spazzo showers alone.

There is something boyish about her body; the female parts seem out of place. There is no softness about her. Over the whole body the flesh is firm and muscular. She looks like an athlete. The discus thrower. As the spazzo moves under the shower, muscles ripple—back, neck, shoulders, stomach, arms, legs. Ridges rise and fall as the voluntary muscles struggle against the resistance of involuntary spastic motions. The big muscle groups are plainly visible at work beneath tight skin.

Tight fingers grip a wet washcloth. The arm straightens, flexing against its own resistance. It drags the washcloth across a bar of soap on the bench beside her. She scrapes the rag over her other arm and bats it at her neck and trunk. Then she leans forward into the falling water. Still holding the limp cloth, she tries to stick up one leg.

With that effort, the spazzo loses control. One arm and one leg jerk out, and the hand sends the soap flying off the bench. As the soap continues its trajectory across the wet tile floor, a counselor crouches down and catches it on the fly.

It is truly an elegant catch. A nude, perfect body crouches, knees and hips bending in perfect harmony, heels rising from the floor to touch her buttocks, weight shifting to the balls of her feet. At the same instant, her toes spread out and press the floor with unbearable loveliness, a slender arm instinctively reaches out, and perfect fingers scoop up the soap. Just as gracefully, she stands up, her feet firmly planted on the floor. She takes three long steps, then leans over in an arabesque and drops the soap on the bench from which it was shot.

The spazzo looks up and grins a silly grin of thanks. It is the same grin I always see in photographs of myself. The natural grin of a spazzo. And then I know: That absurd body is exactly like my own.

The rest of the room no longer exists in my consciousness. The familiar noises of the bathroom—human voices talking, laughing, hollering, showers running, johns flushing, the screen door slamming—merge into an indistinct din. My whole self concentrates on the image of the spazzo, wet and shiny under harsh fluorescent lights.

Whether it takes hours or seconds, I can't say: The spazzo finishes her shower. The perfect girl counselor comes to help the spazzo from the shower to her chair. As the counselor supports her, the spazzo presses her feet onto the floor to stand up. The counselor wraps a beautiful arm around the spazzo's back and walks with stately, measured steps.

I can't take my eyes off their feet. The counselor's feet caress the wet tile floor. Every movement asserts confidence, comfort, and control. Those feet are at home in the world. Beside them are two alien feet, strangers stomping against the tile. The parts of those feet don't work together. The spazzo carries all her weight right on her heels. The ankles are completely rigid. The toes stick up. They are the feet of a fool.

Watching it in motion, I despise that spazzo's body and my own. The normal girl's body is made up of lovely curves, a perfection of balance and proportion. Her movements reflect the harmony of her physical composition. She produces arcs and waves as she moves. Separate movements flow elegantly into a whole action; it's like music. She'd be a worthy subject for a great artist. The spazzo is nothing but straight lines and angles. Her pieces move separately and sequentially, when she can get them to move at all. For her portrait a stick figure would do.

By the time the spazzo plops into her wheelchair, the air, normally hot and steamy as a sauna, has been transformed. It is electric. A powerful energy is at work, but not the kind of force that knocks its objects flat or blows them to bits. Rather, its action is invisible. I am the object of two opposing forces in perfect equilibrium, a magnetism borne of fascination and horror. Thus attracted and repelled, suspended between two poles, I am powerless to move. It could be called inertia. But, sitting still and silent, I am hardly a body at rest.

"She's all right now," Sue says. I jump. I am confused. Denise. The seizure. Oh, yes. As Sue pushes me toward an empty shower, I feel ashamed.

I try not to think how I look when Sue removes the

towel and walks me, heel-heel-heel-heel, into the shower, my knees bent, my toes curled. I let Sue scrub me; better not to move. I try to feel the warm water and just be. Soon taps will sound.

Just after lights-out, my powers of self control fail me. I lie in bed and try every trick I know—everything that has ever worked in the past—but I can't clear my mind of the image of that body, of my own body. I cannot stop despising that body.

I can't stop thinking that whoever sees my naked body sees those clumsy lines and angles. I've always assumed that I will get married one day. Now I question whether a man will ever want to touch that body—or, if he does, whether I could allow it.

I think again of a romantic fantasy I lifted from my favorite soap opera. My boyfriend and I are finishing dinner in an elegant restaurant. He puts a diamond ring on my finger, looks soulfully into my eyes, and orders champagne. Many times I've imagined this scene, with many variations. At first the guy was the handsome young intern in the soap opera; later, he was a famous actor or singer; once, when I was a freshman, I even dared to think about the best-looking guy in the senior class. But usually he's been someone I haven't met yet, someone I'll meet at Chapel Hill. He's always been handsome, and always normal.

But now I realize something: I've left myself out of my own fantasy. Abandoning the struggle to clear my mind, I take up a more desperate struggle—to reconceive the fantasy with myself, as I really am, in the female lead.

I decide to play it with the original leading man, the handsome intern. But right away he turns into someone else. He's the surfer guy, that expert shagger. And this time, the story doesn't start when dinner ends.

The story begins with him pushing me into the restaurant. People turn to look at us, because he's so cute and I'm crippled, and crippled people aren't typically part of the in-crowd in fancy restaurants. When we order, the waitress doesn't understand me. He translates. The steaming plates of food arrive. He cuts up my meat and feeds me the first bite. He wipes my chin with the cloth napkin.

"It's nice to see you and your sister out, having a nice time," the old lady at the next table says.

His eyes spark with amusement. "Some people!" he whispers. Our true relationship is our special secret.

He makes witty conversation. I try not to snort my food. When he gives me the ring, I almost have a spaz attack. He pulls my fingers straight to get the ring on. We wrap our fingers together, and I squeeze tight. It's like when we dance the shag. His hand is warm and strong. So is mine. The old lady is looking at us again. Surprised.

The champagne comes. He puts a straw in my glass, but the glass is too shallow and the straw falls out. He anchors it with a tea spoon. We drink to a long and happy life together.

The fantasy doesn't work. Obviously, this handsome guy can have his pick of the girls at Chapel Hill or Wrightsville Beach. He can have any of the camp counselors, with their perfect bodies and miraculous fingers and toes. What's he doing with a camper? Is he kinky?

No, I tell myself, he loves me for myself. He must.

We're on our honeymoon. He has to help me on the toilet, but his wonderful sense of humor makes everything fine.

We get in bed. He wraps his arms around me.

Lying flat on my army cot, I can almost feel his warmth, the pressure of his body against mine. Under my mattress the springs groan. My legs are jerking; an early sign of a spaz attack. I'm afraid I might wake the campers sleeping around me—or even Carole and Sue in their cubicle. I need to divert my mind, but I can't. Somehow I manage to hold my body still, but my mind keeps going.

He is crawling over me. I want him with all my heart and soul, but my body tries to fight him off. I feel him recoil, but then he starts again, like someone determined to get a job done. He pushes himself between my legs. I kick and knock his wind out. Again. Just like in the canoe. I'm almost sick.

"I don't want to force you," he says. He does love me.

"Go ahead." My voice sounds weird. He's not really

forcing me; he's just forcing my body. My body's trying to escape, but *I* want him, I really do. He knows that. We wrestle. He dodges my punches and kicks; finally he pins my legs with his legs and shoves my arms out of his way. Now he can get to me, with his mouth, with the one hand that isn't holding me down. I'm frantic, and he's not making it any better. It takes all his strength and his dancer's agility, but finally, he does what needs to be done. Relief. It's over.

I know sex is possible, but I can't imagine it giving pleasure. Not to me. Not with my body the way it really is.

I stare up at the blackness around the rafters and try to come up with a new fantasy. What if it's not a normal guy? Maybe a CP guy. A CP guy could love me just the way I am. A spaz attack wouldn't bother him. Together, we could figure everything out. But where would we live? Who would feed and dress us? Even in fantasy, two CPs can't make enough money to have live-in help.

What about someone like Willie? A hideous guy might see beauty in a strong, muscular girl. After all, what's wrong with muscles? Who decided all women have to be soft? He can help me. He's already fed me—a hot dog—quite capably. He's a very good guy, and going to college. We could laugh together. He's patient. With him I could relax.

But I'm not ready for that idea.

Willie belongs with someone like Sara, if only she'd

have him. He should be with a rebel, someone who doesn't give a rip what people think. For me, marrying someone like Willie would mean giving up the treasured place I've won in the normal world. I've never had a boyfriend, but I love going out with my crowd. Whenever we pile into a car to go to the movies or get burgers, I'm proud to be with a group of healthy, good-looking people. I feel like somebody. Maybe that's petty and vain, maybe I'm kidding myself, but I'm not ready to give it up. I'm not ready to join the leper colony. I'm not ready to be half of a couple who turns people's stomachs.

Over and over again, I try to rein in my thoughts and go to sleep, but thoughts rush like an emotional spaz attack. Somehow, I have to get control; I have no other choice.

No one can help me.

Not my family. No way could I talk to my dad. Cindy would tell me to talk to Mom, but Mom would be at a complete loss—and in such pain. I could never do that to her. My girlfriends would smile and give me pep talks and hugs, but behind my back they'd exchange sad looks. Telling them would only make things worse.

I could tell Sara. With her I can talk freely. But she has already worked out her solution: be an old maid and die young. It's a dignified, and achievable, solution. But it doesn't seem right, even for her. And it certainly isn't right for me. I'm not one of Jerry's kids; I'll have a long life. And I don't want a long life alone.

But tonight I am alone. No one can help.

It is closer to reveille than to taps when I am finally too tired to think. I turn over and the sheets knot themselves around my feet. My right hand draws up into a fist, and my thumb snags my hair. My face is mashed into the blue and white mattress ticking. I lie like I've fallen from some great height.

Equilibrium may be disturbed by the increase of one force or, equally, by the decrease of the countervailing force.

I am tired. I am so filled with tiredness that there's no room inside me for anything else. Carole puts a plate in front of me. Two sausage patties, glistening with grease. A square of scrambled eggs as dense as the yellow sponge that sits on the ledge above my mom's kitchen sink. I shake my head.

"You don't feel like eating? Is it the wrong time of the month, maybe?" Carole whispers. "My stomach always gets queasy right before it starts. You want to try some toast, maybe?"

I take a bite. I've never felt this way before. Off balance. Not myself. What if I get stuck? What if I never go back to being my same old self? That would be horrible. Maybe. Or maybe not. Maybe it's time to change, time to face facts. The toast sticks in my throat going down.

Sara sips her coffee and tries to lure me into an

argument about the Bible. I can't rouse myself even to be annoyed.

"Sa-ra, I don't feel too good. It's the wrong time of the month." My period is due in a little less than a week. It seems a useful excuse. Sara gives me a sympathetic look— and silence.

The sausage is too much, but I force down the toast and eggs. When the food hits bottom, I feel somewhat better. Not the same, but better. Maybe I can endure the day.

We roll off the path onto the grass behind the lodge. Already it must be up in the high eighties; just the thought of outdoor sports exhausts me. I guess I could report sick, but I'm not really sick.

Sara says, "I have an idea."

Oh, no. An idea.

She indicates Denise and Peggy Jo. "They were talking about badminton. We can say they're playing proxy for us and just sit around. As long as we cheer a little, we'll be left alone, especially since you're feeling cruddy."

She does know how to work the system, and right now I'm glad. I'm glad she's helping, not trying to stir something up. I stare vacantly and let her get things organized. The game starts, and I make the effort to sit up straight, the way an interested person would sit.

She looks at me with the corner of her eye. "You do the telethons, I know."

I nod.

"Easter Seals, right?"

"Yes. And CP too."

"I've never done one. What's it like?"

"Oh, pretty inter-esting. I've met some ath-letes and a soap star. That was neat."

"I guess it would be. But sometimes don't you get aggra-vated? You know, they make such big high drama out of everything."

My head follows the ball, but I don't really see it. "Last time, I was inter-viewed with my dad. He bragged on me. He said I was a jun-ior mar-shall, Be-ta club. Per-fect atten-dance, lots of friends." I shrug.

"Yeah?"

"I felt good. My pa-rents were proud. I thought I had a posi-tive mes-sage. Then, the MC looked into the cam-era, with tears—" My voice is almost a squeak. I'm not sure I can finish the story.

"Tears in his eyes? What did he say?" She leans forward.

"He said, 'Friends, this girl needs speech thera-py.'"

She starts to interrupt, but now I'm determined to fin-ish. "He said, 'With-out your help, she won't get it.'"

Sara throws her head back. "What a complete and total asshole!"

I laugh. I can't believe I'm laughing. Until this moment, I saw nothing funny about it. After it happened, I tried to put it out of my mind, but instead I kept getting stuck, asking myself what I could have done to make my point better. Now laughter has broken the logjam and is washing over my brain, carrying away the trash.

Sara is thoughtful. "That's a classic telethon story. The idiot couldn't see it—you're a speech-therapy success story. As good as it gets." She studies the tangle of trees on the other end of the field. "Or else he was scratching around for an angle to get the phones lit up. Never mind that it's false. And insulting."

I'm engaged, thinking again. "Some-times, I wish we didn't have tele-thons."

"Yeah."

"But with-out the tele-thon, this camp would-n't be here."

"Exactly. It wouldn't."

She turns back to the badminton game. "Who's playing for who, anyway?"

"I've got De-nise."

"Naturally—she's ahead. I shouldn't have asked!"

I raise my left eyebrow. I have good control of that eyebrow. The sun has moved so high that the shadows of two pines over our heads shrink to mere polka dots. Poor Denise and Peggy Jo are soaked with sweat.

"You know," Sara says, "there are a lot of telethon stories around here. I've been collecting them. People do telethons, year after year. And each year it seems they get more uncomfortable."

I nod.

"There are exceptions. Impossible dreamers like Dolly and maybe the aussies—who can tell?—some people love the telethon, genuinely. But most of us are just pretending. We keep our feelings hidden, even from ourselves. Underground. Under cover. And it's our silence, our cooperation, that keeps the whole structure in place. Withdraw that support and it all falls down."

She pauses. There's nothing to say, but I feel my head nod.

"So," she says with dancing eyes, "I've been working on a little scheme. A small conspiracy."

What now?

"I've been thinking we should make a real statement at Talent Night. Bag 'Morning at Camp Courage.' Do something meaningful. Guerrilla theater. A reverse telethon."

"A what?"

"It's a futuristic fantasy. A world where cripples are in control. Nothing like it has ever been done here. Nothing at all like it. Amazing, huh? It'll blow the lid off."

"Ta-lent Night is to-night. We have a skit prepared. It's funny."

"Yeah, but switching will be no problem. I've got it all figured out. Mary and Dolly can do the same stuff we've been rehearsing. Everyone else is adaptable. I'll be the MC. I've told everyone their parts and cues. I wasn't sure of your part, till just now. Now I've got it. You'll be cohost. You just nod, nod at everything, nod, nod, nod, until I say, 'What do you think of that, Jean?' That's your cue. 'What do you think of that, Jean?' When you hear that, you say, 'That girl needs speech therapy.' It'll be hilarious. Believe me!"

"The o-thers know a-bout this?"

"Yes. I've been talking it around since I got here."

I think about the serious-looking discussions she's been having with Peggy Jo, Denise, Yvonne, even Margie—always out of my earshot. "Why did-n't you tell me?"

"I had to be sure I could trust you."

"TRUST me?"

"I saw those telethon souvenirs you brought, and I fig-ured you'd be hard to recruit." It's like she's talking about someone else, someone who doesn't matter much. "But after last night, I decided you'd be ready."

Last night? How can she possibly know?

"Last night they showed they have no respect for us. What we think doesn't count." She's talking about the movie. *Pollyanna*. That seems so long ago.

"The Soviet tried to play their game, within their rules. But then they repealed the rules. So, I decided, defini-tively, out in front of the lodge last night, that we'd do the reverse telethon. Everyone's for it. It'll be tremendous. The Jaycees and the Honorable State Senator McNeill—all the Philistine elite—will be gathered here to gawk at us with no idea what's about to hit them."

Sue comes to check on us. "How's it going out here?"

"Fine," we say in unison.

As Sue stands by, we attend to the badminton game. Peggy Jo and Denise come over for coaching. My energy rises; Sara's scheme has me a little keyed up. I'm hungry now.

Sue stays until the game ends. "It's great to see you all working so well together."

Peggy Jo leans down, ostensibly to hit my brakes. She barely moves her lips. "I hear you're in!" Carole comes with life vests, and Peggy Jo drops her things on the sand and dashes to the water. Now that I know, I can see Sara passing messages all day. The reverse telethon is on. Jean's in.

Carole, so cute in her demure two-piece swimsuit, holds my shoulders. We walk into the water, and I try to remember. Did I ever say "I'm in"? No. No one asked. Am I in? I'm not sure. I'm still tired.

I feel my steel-awl heels puncture the sand. In my mind I can see Carole's feet alongside mine, leaving gentle impressions with each step as they lead our two bodies forward. The water reaches my chest, and I lie back.

I try to let the water carry me, but I'm too off-center. If I don't get moving, I might sink. I kick and propel myself headfirst all the way to the floating barrels. Here I stop. I have left everyone behind. The nagging stress is giving way to wild thoughts, doubts are rising to despair. Do I have a place, anywhere, in the world?

I have to stop it. I can't relax, so I hold back my wild impulses with countertension. I force myself to worry about the reverse telethon.

I don't really understand Sara's plan. Whatever it is, it'll probably fail. But when it fails, I don't want it to be my fault. I'll be cool. For the rest of the day I'll go through the motions; when the time comes, I'll fall in line. Whatever that means.

I push off against a barrel and start kicking again. I'll go with the script. Sara's script. The script no one else knows anything about.

It might be a terrible thing.

I kick against the cold black water until a sharp pain grabs my stomach. Good. The pain is better than what's waiting in the back of my mind, ready to take over if I give it a chance.

"YOU GOTTA GET UP, you gotta get up, you gotta get up this morning!" They stand like soldiers: Peggy Jo in the baggy St. Andrew's T-shirt, Denise in Sue's Camp Courage shirt with the crutch-and-pine logo.

We all groan. It's the opening of "Morning at Camp Courage."

"Okay," Sara says. "Now groan real big. Everyone has to get it right away, even the PMRs in the back row."

The period before supper is reserved for final rehearsals. Through the screens, we hear the competition declaiming lines, singing in chorus and solo, strumming guitars. We're curious, but we can't stop to listen. I'm still tense, unsettled, but now it feels like excitement.

Denise blows an earsplitting whistle and bawls out orders, half camp counselor, half football coach. Peggy Jo pleads ineffectually and struggles with recalcitrant hair clips. It's going very well, but still Sara makes changes. She draws a giant thermometer and adds jokes about the heat. Is this really the decoy skit? After all this work, surely we'll just do this one and forget about whatever it is Sara has schemed up.

"We need Dolly in her party clothes," Sara says.

"Shouldn't y'all be in nightclothes?" Carole asks.

"Yeah, really we should, but I don't want to go to supper in my gown, and changing is such a hassle."

"We could pretend to be under sheets at the beginning," Margie says.

"Perfect!" Sara says. In the corner, Mary is tearing toilet paper with aussie single-mindedness. "He loves me, he loves me not . . ."

"I've gotta hit the bathroom," Carole says. "If y'all don't mind? Okay?" She sounds so much like Peggy Jo's imitation that we all laugh. "Now, y'all? Stop it? Please?"

Sara has another idea. "Let's make Dolly a tiara, like a beauty queen." She flashes her most engaging smile. "Sue, could you possibly run up to the lodge for some aluminum foil?"

"Sure."

As soon as Sue and Carole are out of earshot, Sara asks quietly, "Y'all know your cues?" They all nod. It's on.

"He loves me, he loves me not," Mary drones.

"Just perk up when you hear your name. The positions are the same as 'Morning at Camp Courage,' but we won't be covering up with sheets. Margie'll use the thermometer. I need it marked at ten, and then at forty, and then at one hundred."

"I can do that," Peggy Jo says.

"Okay, mark it at ten now, and after she uses it the first time, she'll bring it back to you to mark again."

"Margie, you sure you can remember those numbers?" Sara asks.

"Can I look at the thermometer?"

"Sure. That's the idea."

"Then I just believe I can."

"Yvonne, what's the news?"

"We're definitely going last. Plan A."

"Great! I knew you'd pull it off; they'd never suspect you as a conspirator!"

I shoot off a questioning eyebrow, and Yvonne fills me in. "I convinced Sue that our skit was so good that we just had to go last. Sue convinced Mr. Bob!"

"What was Plan B?" Peggy Jo asks.

"To have someone hide in the bathroom, so whenever they call us, we wouldn't be ready to go on."

"Man, I'm glad we didn't have to do that," Denise says.

"Really," Sara says. "There was a risk of exposing the gap in surveillance." I look puzzled. "They think they're watching the bathroom, because they come in and out, but they don't pay attention to how long you're in there. Or even *if* you're in there." She looks pointedly at Yvonne.

Yvonne giggles. Maybe that's how she used to sneak off with her CP boyfriend. "Plan B might've made them notice how we hide out. We couldn't have that!"

When Carole returns from the bathroom, we're back into "Morning at Camp Courage." It's going without a hitch. On the floor there is an impressive pile of toilet paper squares.

As soon as I roll into the lodge for the evening program, I feel it. They're here. Outsiders. Visitors from the normal world, the world I came from, the world where Crips get gawked at. The Jaycees and their families have arrived.

A little girl points at me. "What's wrong with her?" A mom with a Laura Petrie hairdo and pea-green shirt pulls down the child's hand and whispers something in her ear. The girl gawks more discreetly, out of the corners of her eyes, and I know I've just witnessed a child learning to gawk like a grown-up.

Mr. Bob is buzzing around a big barrel-chested man in

golf clothes. Without a doubt, it's the Honorable State Senator B. J. McNeill. Introductions are made, backs slapped. Gruff male laughter breaks through the pleasantries.

But in another instant it's like some vital element has been sucked from the air. The state senator's smile has gone glassy, his glad hand gone brittle in midshake. It has to be Willie. Only Willie does that to people! Reactions roll over the crowd; the visitors' faces reflect Willie's movements as clearly as any mirror could. Shock. Horror. Withdrawal. Above the happy Banlon shirts, faces go chalky. I turn my head and find Willie, just where those faces tell me he'd be.

He walks straight to the Honorable State Senator, flashes his terrifying grin, extends his twisted right hand, and introduces himself with the easy affability of—of State Senator McNeill himself, before State Senator McNeill had ever seen Willie or imagined the possible existence of anyone like Willie. Lacking a handy hole to crawl into, the senator stands ramrod-straight. Just as straight, he looks at Willie or, really, looks through Willie, through the screens behind Willie, all the way to the flagpole outside. Willie lets flow a stream of palaver and a river of blather and puffs of guff—all of which give the senator plenty of time to decide what to do about that offered handshake. Ignore it, that's what. Willie pauses to allow the senator to regain the power of speech. "Why. Fine. Thank you. Glad to be here. Heh-heh. Very glad. Very glad indeed." He's found his smile again, his resonant voice, his manly chuckle. But it's all so strained, more like a parody than the real thing. At this stage, Willie's senator act is better than the senator's own.

I bet it's an encounter the senator will never forget. He will probably recover, even to the point of going back to Raleigh and telling his cohorts all about Willie's Courage and Determination and Sadly Significant Deformities. He'll never know what I know. Willie is having a little fun. Giving the senator a scare. Boo!

Now the lodge is full. Mr. Bob escorts the senator to the front row then stands facing the crowd. "Good evening, everyone, and welcome State Senator McNeil, our good friends the Jaycees, and the Jaycee families." They give their parade-float waves, and, yes, Senator McNeill's brave, quickly recovering wave is the best, just like Willie, scorned and covered with scars.

"Before we start, I want to congratulate *everyone*. We're going to see all kinds of talent. We need to keep in mind that everyone is making a contribution and everyone is doing their best. Tonight, every single camper is a star!"

Not again!

Something rises up in me. Like a thick liquid, it fills my stomach, permeates my flesh, penetrates my bones. It's the same substance that poisoned my sleep last night. Last night, though, it was a slow ooze inside me; now it's building with more force than I can absorb; it feels like I'm on the edge of a full-body explosion. It's rage. This must be rage.

It's rage against Mr. Bob, and rage against all the Mr. Bobs of the world. They are to blame. They make us assume, expect, hope. And then they take it all away.

Everyone's a winner; no one's a winner.

I'm just like a normal girl; just like, but not. Not now. Not ever.

I want to give them pain. I want to rip away their assumptions, their expectations, their hopes. I want to do something to them.

My hands have formed themselves into fists, ready to punch. No. To do something, I need control. I will away a spaz attack. I've made up my mind. I want to do the reverse telethon. No matter how bad it may be, it will be no worse than they deserve.

The first skit is derived from *The Beverly Hillbillies*. I watch with half an eye. I'm in, I want to tell Sara. Let's do it. Don't chicken out!

It's all up to her. If she decides to start "Morning at Camp Courage," there's nothing I can do. I look to her for a clue, a signal, but she pretends to be wholly absorbed in the show. Another cabin, another skit, this time sad routines from *Rowan and Martin's Laugh-In*. She laughs at the Henry Gibson poem, groans over Tiny Tim—not the

crippled one but the one with the high-pitched voice—
and claps politely when the act ends.

I make myself watch. There are singers, solo and in
chorus. The deaf camper signs while another sings and
plays the guitar. There's the Motown falsetto I heard at
the campfire. Not at all bad. Other acts are downright
embarrassing. The blind girl sings in a flat mountain
twang, "I fayund my three-hee-yul, own Blueberry Hee-
yul." An overweight, moonfaced MR girl is sheer agony in
tap shoes. Willie lurks discreetly in the background as
some guys in his cabin sing "Michael, Row the Boat
Ashore," and Robert stands apart in his invisible phone
booth, dialing persons unknown, maybe in Goldsboro.
Another Jaycee child points and another Jaycee mother
pulls the pointing finger down. Staring. Looking away. My
rage flares anew. I want to do something. I stop watching
the show and concentrate on revenge. I am waiting, hoping, expecting that revenge will come. Surely Sara will
organize some revenge.

Then some distraction breaks through. It's silence. The
quad has taken the stage. He is sitting up there in front of
us, all alone in his big power chair. People are still and
hushed as though something amazing is happening.

But nothing is happening. The quad is breathing, that's
all. Behind the mouth controls, his face is almost invisible
at this angle. Behind the brace that buttresses him from

tail to chin, there isn't much to see. So what's he up to, up there, all by himself? Willie and Sara obviously know. They're huddled together in their knowingness, cutting looks at me because I don't know.

The quad pulls a deep breath through his nose and opens his mouth. He lets his voice come. Now I know. He's the Broadway baritone. From a withered body and a caved-in chest comes a voice that soars. He is singing "On the Street Where You Live" from *My Fair Lady*, and the rage that was making a combustion inside me gives way to that voice.

Each note is true, the emotion just right—strong and sure, with just the right touch of diffident charm.

Does he know how amazing it is? How strange? He must know. But he doesn't care. He's simply singing. He loves to sing. And why shouldn't he? It's beautiful.

The initial surprise—the freakish spectacle—fades away; the voice is what matters. I listen.

> *People stop and stare,*
> *They don't bother me*
> *For there's nowhere in the world*
> *where I would rather be . . .*

I catch Willie's eye, and he gives me the smile that's no longer repugnant. I know he'll add that verse to his reper-toire and sing it with his special irony. But there is no irony in the singing now. No impurity. Just lovely grace and elegance.

The Jaycees jump to their feet. "Bravo!" State Senator McNeill is out of his mind, harumphing amazement. There's a general roar, and I roar too, as proud as if I'd done the singing myself. The quad has taken over, made them powerless to pretend. Everyone a star? No way. He's the star. They have to admit it. He's better than anyone, better than them for sure. They've been beaten. Beaten bad.

But not bad enough. Not yet.

Another skit and my resolve builds. The counselors feed the campers their lines, and Mr. Bob, personally, has to lead the cheers to try to get these inept performers as much attention as the great quad singer.

"Y'all ready?" Carole asks. There is no one else left.

They get our wheelchairs and Mary into position for "Morning at Camp Courage." I might jump out of my skin. Denise stands on the side. "We got it. Y'all can sit down."

Peggy Jo sets the bedsheets on the floor. It is on. Probably. Only Sara knows for sure. I want to ask, but I hold back; I'm not sure I can talk right now.

Sara bows toward Mr. Bob. "Fearless Leader." She looks straight at the state senator. "Distinguished Philistine high officials, benefactors, staff—"

The voice is strong, clear, deadly serious. She's obviously nervous. I force myself to listen. "Counselors—and comrades." It's on, definitely on. I suppress a squeal.

"It is the year 2030. Twenty years ago we Cripples took control. In the first, violent days of our revolution, our only thought was to punish those who had oppressed us for thousands of years. But now we have matured. We have compassion for those who are different. We raise money to help them."

Sue and Carole exchange puzzled looks. The speech is going too long. We're losing the MRs. Let's get into it, Sara.

"So tonight, ladies and gentlemen, we WELCOME YOU to the third annual Telethon to Stamp Out Normalcy. Applause, please!"

We clap, just like phone people on the telethon. Because we clap, the audience applauds. The aussies clap like robot clapping machines. From the visitors comes polite, befuddled applause. They're definitely confused. My squeal bursts forth.

"Good evening. I'm Sara, your telethon host. With me is my cohost, Jean." I remember to nod. "We have a great show lined up. Jean, are you ready to raise some money— and Stamp Out Normalcy?" I nod.

"Okay, let's get going! Our first guest is Dolly. Dolly is a beauty queen and authoress who has given tirelessly of her time and talents to benefit our cause."

Dolly acknowledges the introduction by kicking one high-heeled foot high up into the air like some sick nightmare Rockette. "Dolly represents our ideal in beauty, and what's more important is her dedication to service. Dolly, tell the telethon audience what this cause means to you."

From her corner, Dolly prattles incoherently to the ceiling. The aluminum foil crown is crushed on one side. The visitors don't understand a word; the rest of us know she's drifted into the usual monologue about her novella. The boys in the back row hoot. But the visitors sit there and smile as they've smiled through every embarrassing moment so far. It's agony, wonderful agony: it's killing Mr. Bob, the counselors, and the guests. And there's no stopping her. She's still blabbing when Peggy Jo drags her away.

Sara smiles her most unctuous smile and looks up to heaven. "What a beautiful person, to give so much of herself to help those who are less fortunate. Truly beautiful in every way. Let's give Dolly a round of applause."

We clap. The visitors clap. They still think that's the thing to do. Idiots!

"Now let's meet Mary. Mary is a telethon booster with a unique fund-raising idea. She calls it a toilet-paper-tear-athon. She plans to set the world record for nonstop toilet paper tearing and has asked sponsors to pledge a penny for every square she rips."

Yvonne crouches behind Mary, hands her the roll of toilet paper, and starts her up. When Sara stops talking, Mary is underway: "He loves me, he loves me not." All her resources—mental, physical, spiritual—are given over to separating those squares. "He loves me, he loves me not."

We cheer. Mary keeps at her work. "He loves me, he loves me not." The little squares glide gracefully to the floor. "He loves me, he loves me not."

"Throughout our show, we'll be watching those pennies, symbolized by wafting squares of toilet paper, pile up. Mary's an inspiration to all of us. Right, Jean?" I nod. My left arm punches the air. Almost imperceptibly, Sara dodges.

"He loves me, he loves me not, he loves me, he loves me not." I try not to get too tickled. I want to be a good second banana.

"Ladies and gentlemen," Sara leans forward dramatically. "Those phones aren't ringing. How can we Stamp Out Normalcy unless we get those phones ringing? You've got to give.

"All of you out there, if you have a normal child or grandchild, you know the importance of this cause. Please call and give what you can.

"And if you have a crippled child, have you ever thought, 'There, but for the grace of God, go I'? It's true. Normalcy can strike any family. You should light up these phone lines in celebration of your good fortune, and thank God for your crippled child! Right, Jean?"

I nod and wish with all my heart that it were true. Thank God for crippled children!

"If we can stamp out normalcy in this generation, all our children will be safe from this dreadful scourge." I nod a great big nod they can see in the back row. The state senator whispers in Mr. Bob's ear.

"Hey, our operators are busy now!" Yvonne and Margie pretend to talk on the telephone. "This is beautiful."

I nod.

"Margie, how are we doing?"

Margie hangs up her invisible phone and holds up the picture of the thermometer. "Sara, our goal is one hundred thousand." She studies the thermometer, marked at ten. "We have raised—ten." A triumphant Margie leads the applause. I think Mr. Bob's face is red, although I can't tell for sure, not at this distance in yellow bug lights. Margie sits down, pleased with herself and her long speech.

"That's a terrific start, but we need to do better to lick this problem. Right, Jean?"

I nod.

"He loves me, he loves me not."

"Now, ladies and gentlemen, it's time to meet someone very special, one of the unfortunate people we are here to help. Peggy Jo!"

She walks out, pulls up a folding chair, and shakes

hands with Sara. "I know it takes a lot of courage to come out here. Tell the people why you're doing it."

She sits down and crosses her legs. "Well, I want to help find a cure. I'd give anything to be like everyone else." She pretends to wipe away a tear.

Sara squeezes her arm. "Tell the people what it's like to live with a horrible condition like normalcy."

"It's rough at times. Wherever you go, people stare at you. You're always different. I'm used to it now, but it was really hard when I was a kid. When I tried to make friends in school, the other kids used to call me names."

"Like what?"

"Walkie-talkie," Peggy Jo sobs. Laughter bursts from the campers.

"Children can be so cruel."

"It's fear and ignorance, I know that now," Peggy Jo says through her tears, "but that doesn't make it any easier. I want what other girls want. I dream of going down the aisle someday with a gorgeous guy—a guy like Willie."

Willie stands up and blows her a kiss, exactly as Cary Grant might do it, if Cary Grant were ghastly. Peggy Jo can't manage her next line.

"But it is not to be, unless a cure is found," Sara covers. "I know you're all choked up."

I squeal but stay in control.

"Peggy Jo, I promise you, we will never forget your

courage. We'll do everything we can to find a cure so that someday you'll be just like us."

She staggers away.

"Jean, I know all the folks out there were touched by Peggy Jo's story." I nod. A little clumsy nod, I feel. "Margie, how're we doing?"

"Thanks to Peggy Jo's courage, we are now at forty thousand dollars!" She holds the thermometer way over her head.

"HOW ABOUT THAT???" Cheers go up. I'm delighted. Margie is doing so well.

"Now I want to tell you about Yvonne." Hearing her cue, Yvonne strides across the stage like Miss America. "If you saw last year's telethon, you know Yvonne is one of our great success stories. She was born with two legs."

I manage to shake my head sadly.

"But, thanks to brilliant surgeons, she's down to one. She still walks with an artificial leg, but no one would call her a walkie-talkie anymore. She's earned the right to be called a cripple. Just like any of us. And she has high hopes, hopes of getting a wheelchair someday. With your help, I think she can do it!"

Kick the leg off! my brain yells.

"I know I can!" Yvonne says with a thumbs-up. "Someday I'll get in that chair!"

Drop it! Show them the stump! Give them a real good look!

"That's the spirit," Sara says.

I nod. Yvonne's part is done, and she walks away on her plastic leg. Too bad.

"He loves me, he loves me not."

"Now let's meet someone who is not so fortunate, at least not yet. Come on out, Denise!" Denise kneels before us and kisses our hands. "Denise is terribly afflicted. She can walk, run, even dance. She thinks normally. She looks soooo normal." Sara shudders a little. "But she never lets it get her down. Tell us, Denise."

"My philosophy is to focus on my disabilities, not my abilities. I mean, like, it's true I can think, but not like Albert Einstein. I'm strong, but not like Muhammad Ali. There are other people much more able than me. So compared to them, I'm a Crip. I try to be positive." Jaycees and Jaycee-ettes are whispering, making sure they've heard it right. The campers are agog.

"Wow, that really makes you think, right, Jean?" I nod. "Denise, tell us what you have done with your life, despite the bad hand you've been dealt."

"Well, I went to school. And now I have a job. It's in a sheltered workshop with other people like me. We weave baskets, stuff envelopes, and string beads. I'll never make enough to get off Ability Benefits, but I'm proud to have a job. It makes me feel almost like a Crip."

"Denise, you're an inspiration. Sometimes we Crips find that things come too easy. We go to the best schools, and we get the best jobs. Because we run the world." Sara pauses and in the audience the Motown falsetto shouts amen. "We take it all for granted. It takes someone like you to make us thankful."

"God bless us, every one." Denise genuflects, and Sara gives her a pat on the head.

"Jean, give the people your reaction to Denise's story. What do you think of that, Jean?"

I know it's my cue, but I can only stutter. I've forgotten my line. Now I remember, but too late. I'm too flustered to get it out.

The silence continues, and finally I get it out: "That girl needs speech THER-a-py." It's incomprehensible, but Sara looks completely satisfied.

She looks to the audience. "Jean has hit the nail on the head. As usual. Friends, comrades, Philistines, did you hear what she said?"

"No!" shouts one of the boys in the back.

I repeat. I struggle to say it better, but I'm so nervous. They still don't get it. My eyes tell Sara, Please don't make me say it again.

Okay, she seems to answer, I'll take care of it. "She said"—Sara speaks as slow as a foreign-language tape— "That girl needs speech therapy." She waits for the reaction. Among the staff and visitors there is uncomfortable silence. The Norms go rigid, stone-faced. But the campers are tittering. Now, they're laughing. Finally. Mr. Bob stands up. Furious. But I am jubilant. The joke worked. My heavy CP accent made it work.

Sara looks at me. "Yes, Denise desperately needs speech therapy. And without your help, ladies and gentlemen, she won't get it."

For me, hearing those words repeated is a kind of exorcism. If only that asshole from the telethon could be here!

Mr. Bob heads toward Sue and Carole. They stand up to meet him in the aisle.

"He loves me, he loves me not."

"Imagine living with all the pain Denise must feel. Imagine never fitting in, anywhere. A round peg in a square hole." Mr. Bob is sputtering. Sue looks defensive, then stern. Carole rubs her hair the way she does when she's perplexed. Sara keeps on talking.

"Give generously, and we will never have to worry about the birth of another normal child. What a great world that would be!"

Now Mr. Bob, Sue, and Carole stand side by side like a row of bowling pins, powerless to stop what's rolling toward them. And in a way they are. Stopping the skit would create a scene, and Norms are scared of any scene they don't fully control. Go ahead! Shut us down! See what happens! But at the same time I begin to hope Sara will end the skit soon. Anxiety is leaking back into my brain.

"Margie, what's the total?"

"WE REACHED OUR GOAL! ONE HUNDRED

THOUSAND!" She raises the thermometer high in the air. Her excitement is absolutely genuine.

"A NEW RECORD!" Sara says. "We've reached our goal! In the shortest telethon ever! In closing, remember:

When you walk through a storm,
keep your head up high . . ."

We sing loud. More quietly, some of the Crips in the audience join in.

"YOU'LL NEVER WALK ALONE!"

In the reverse telethon, what was a metaphor becomes plain, literal truth. "You'll never walk alone!"

It's over so fast. We haven't even taken our bows, and Mr. Bob is standing in front of us. "Let's clap for *all* of our performers—all the singers and dancers and actors—all who showed Camp Courage spirit tonight!"

They clap. The Honorable State Senator, the Jaycees, the Jaycee-ettes, the Jaycee children. Enthusiastically, almost gratefully, they do what Mr. Bob tells them to do. Then the Crips start to move, as we always move when the evening program is over. I see the surfer guy shaking the state senator's hand and hear the senator's *heh-heh* over the noise of the crowd. It is as though nothing has happened.

Head 'em up, Move 'em out. As Sue unlocks Sara's brakes, she bends down so close that I can smell the shampoo in her hair. She speaks only to Sara. "I'm not saying a word tonight. Mr. Bob will talk to you in the morning."

Sara smiles a satisfied smile. "Fine, fine. I'll look forward to it."

They're trying to rush us out, but it's impossible to rush this many cripples out of a room that has only one normal door. As we file past, Willie gives me a little poke. "Too cool! Speech therapy! You were just great."

The others are still milling around the lodge, and our cabin is halfway down the hill. A knot spazzes in my stomach. What did Sara get us into? I've been feeling so odd and got kind of carried away during the skit. It was so amazing how it all fell into place. But now I need to think. Now it's done, over with, and I need to think. After the fact.

It's dark, but the outdoor lighting will stay on until taps. Under the lights, we make weird overlapping shadows on the path.

I have no desire to talk. I need to think. However, I don't do any thinking. My body hits the cot and the nervous energy that fueled me all day crashes. I'm gone almost as soon as they pull the sheet over me and turn off the lights.

Day Nine

"Are we in trouble?" Margie whispers.

I shrug.

"I think Sara's in trouble. Don't you?"

I nod. Without a doubt, she's in trouble. She vanished with Sue right after breakfast; we know they're in Mr. Bob's little office, getting dressed down. We know, but none of us mentions it. There was no mention during the whole getting-up routine, no mention during breakfast at the lodge. No mention until Margie of all people brings it up.

Margie sits on my footlocker and stares at her sneaker scraping the floor. "I hope Sara's not being punished. It ain't right. We all did it."

Something makes me want to hug her. Her body seems to cry for comfort, a body so worried, wrapped in big happy bands of yellow and blue polyester. But instead of hugging, I grin my silly spastic grin. Margie's face goes light. I sit up straight to say everything will be all right.

She stands up and pushes the broom across the floor for the third time. In the dustpan she collects barely a thimbleful of sand. "No way Mr. Bob going to find sand in this cabin. Not the least little bit."

"Margie," Denise says, "I heard the other cabins leaving a while back. Mr. Bob should be here now. I think he won't be inspecting today."

"That's all right, I reckon."

"Yeah, who needs Mr. Bob anyway?" Denise bobs her head. "Margie, you know more about clean than he ever dreamed of! Just tell me how these blinds look."

Margie hides her face behind her hands, but she can't resist peeking through her fingers at the blinds. They are level all around, with cords coiled like new spools of thread.

"Let's put up all these things," she says. Margie, Denise, and Peggy Jo take toiletries off the window ledges and stow them in footlockers. Finally, Margie sets my teddy bear on my pillow, so straight he could be posing for a portrait.

When the cabin can't get any cleaner, we go outside and Margie sweeps the path.

Near the gangway an oak seedling has sprouted. I count eight leaves. Each leaf spreads as flat as an open hand; the thick, round fingers mirror one another on two sides of the center vein. On a sturdy old bough, those leaves would look right, but instead they are attached to a slender young twig: adult leaves, baby tree. So far as I can tell, this infant oak is alone in the world, no parent in sight. I can't recall seeing any oaks since I've been here. How did one acorn come to fall in this spot?

I imagine the oak growing strong, branching out, reaching for the sky. No. It won't make it. There's no room. It sprouted right on the edge of the asphalt. On the other side, the hillside drops straight down. The next hard rain will wash away the sliver of loose sand and the seedling with it.

I could get Margie to dig it up and plant it in a better spot. But I think not. If I transplant the seedling, I might kill it. Left alone, it will die in due course, by the same accident that caused it to spring where it is.

That will be better.

"You see anything else needs cleaning?" Margie asks.

I shake my head, and we go inside.

We hear the familiar rattle on the gangway. Through the screen door comes Sue's rear end and then Sara's back wheels. They turn into the cabin, and behind them the screen door groans closed.

Sue looks grim. "Sara, you better report to your cabinmates."

"Gladly, Sue." She has the manner of someone who has just stood up at a banquet to make a toast. "Cabinmates: According to Fearless Leader Bob, we performed the Most Inappropriate Skit in Camp Courage History. And from eight years' experience in this place, I can tell you that is no small distinction."

"Sara, don't be so smart," Sue snaps.

"Sorry, I was born that way."

I look down.

"At any rate, I took full responsibility. I told Bob I organized the whole thing. I told him Sue and Carole knew nothing, nothing, nothing. Bob wanted to send me home, but my mother is in Spain, and my grandmother can't take me till tomorrow. So he's stuck with me."

Openly, Margie claps. The others keep silent, but they can't hide the pleasure on their faces.

"Bob says bad campers should experience the 'natural consequences' of our actions. So, he asks me, 'What is the natural consequence of a skit so inappropriate that it turns visiting Philistines—however briefly—into pillars of salt?' I say social disapproval. He says, 'Not enough.'" She waggles her finger like a disapproving kindergarten teacher. Like Mr. Bob. "So I suggest zero points for Talent in the inter-cabin competition. Not enough. So maybe zero points for Camp Spirit, I say. Well, turns out nothing's enough. We're so far ahead in cabin cleanup that we're unbeatable, even without talent or spirit. So Fearless Leader is disqualifying us all together."

Her flip tone goes cold. "Around here, comrades, the

natural consequence of whatever we do is that they do whatever they want. They make the rules. They decide who wins and who loses. They have the power—"

Sue interrupts. "Understand this. What you did embarrassed Carole and me. We looked like we didn't know what was going on in our own cabin. In front of all those visitors, too. This camp wouldn't be here without them, or without the telethon. It was cruel."

"You can't be serious!" Sara sputters. "Cruel?"

Carole sinks down on one of the cots. "Yes, in a way, I have to agree. They felt so good about this camp. We all did. And now? What should we think? How should we feel? It is—painful—you know?"

Last night I wanted to inflict pain. Now I can barely remember why. How could I want to hurt Carole? Or Sue? How could any of us?

"Look. I can't worry about the Jaycees or that red-faced Grand Benefactor or any of you. If it hurt, fine. That means we got heard. But it doesn't matter, really. The show wasn't for y'all. It was for us. I know we're supposed to put on a good face and put up with the telethon and all *that* cruelty, but, hell, I've had enough and—"

Sue interrupts. "Sara, you're leaving something out. Mr. Bob gave you a choice."

"Oh, yes. Right. Bob says I can put us back into the competition. I have the power, he says. All I have to do is apologize."

My heart bounces up. He's ready to forgive. We can still win Best Cabin All Around. We can set things right.

"Thing is, I can't apologize. I'm not sorry."

I look from face to face, but I can't tell what the others are thinking. The silence is making me nuts. I have to say it. "Well, I'm sorry."

"Oh, please," Sara says.

"I wish we did-n't do it. Peo-ple might think we're bit-ter."

"Bitter! Christ Almighty! You can't stand that, huh? The Crosstown Cripple might lose her spot in the Fire Parade." She turns to the others. "She's a regular Norm in Crip's clothing."

They laugh. They all laugh. Denise, Peggy Jo, Yvonne, even Dolly. Margie most of all.

A sob rises in my throat; pressure builds inside my head. I won't cry. I won't give her the satisfaction. I turn my head and study the rippling shades of green outside the screens. I listen, hard, to a squirrel running on the roof.

Sara raises her eyebrows and cuts a little look around the cabin. I wish Becky from arts and crafts weren't taking herself quite so seriously. She's trying so hard to be stern, but it's hard to be stern while cutting crepe paper, wrapping it around cut coat hangers, and gathering it with string. Even harder to be grim while fluffing bright red flower petals.

"Now, be real careful how you wrap the tape. It should overlap, but just barely, and do a triple layer when you get to the base of the flower. Be sure it's tight enough to hold." With clenched teeth and furrowed brow and pony-tails bouncing on both sides of her head, she peels green floral tape off the roll.

"Now I'll show you the leis." She opens a box of rainbow Kleenex and starts pulling. Pink. Blue. Yellow. White. She scowls her worst scowl yet; maybe the Kleenex pop out too cheerfully. She rips the box in half. From the life-less heap she takes a limp tissue and gathers it with sewing thread.

"Those look great, Becky," Sara says, apparently untouched by all that sternness. "Can I see up close how you connect them?"

Becky passes the flowers to her. "Now, we expect you to make centerpieces for all eight tables for the Hawaiian luau tonight. And make as many leis as you can. Mr. Bob will let you come to the banquet and closing ceremonies— if you put in a good day's work."

"We will, definitely." Sara turns to Yvonne. "This camp really does need new decorations. You remember how tawdry the old ones looked last year; I bet by now they're absolutely shot."

I'm exasperated. Doesn't Mr. Bob know Sara is just delighted to stay indoors all day and make flowers? He's thrown Br'er Rabbit right into the briar patch.

"Peggy Jo, let's figure out how much stuff we have."
Sara isn't letting herself be punished; she's taking charge.

"Six big packages of crepe paper. Let's see . . . fifteen
coat hangers. Lots of Kleenex!"

"How many stems can we get from one coat hanger?"

"Three probably," Yvonne says.

"Okay, Jean. You're the math whiz. How many flowers
per table?"

I shrug. I've had enough of Sara's organizing. Her organizing sucked me into the reverse telethon. True, in the excitement of the moment, I wanted to do it. But I never had a chance to say no. I never had a chance to think. She used me. She took advantage of the way I like to go along.

The others try to work out the count. I know there will be six flowers on five tables and five on the other three. But let them figure it out. They make tally marks on paper. I can't believe a big brain like Sara has to make tally marks on paper.

Finally they get it. Now there's a big discussion about the decorations. Should all the centerpieces be the same? What about the odd numbers? What colors would look good together? And then the leis. Endless discussions.

"Who can handle the wire cutters?" Sara asks.

Denise straightens and clips coat hangers. Yvonne and Peggy Jo cut crepe paper. Margie wraps the stems, so even, so tidy. Sara's fingers churn out dainty Kleenex flowers and her mouth churns out endless advice to everyone else.

"Becky, thanks for coming by," she says graciously. "I think we've got it together, so we can let you go to your campers."

I'm flabbergasted that Becky lets Sara dismiss her that way. And Sara obviously finds it amusing. "Well," she says, maybe before Becky is out of earshot, "Becky really has a way with prison labor!"

I can't make flowers so I'll just sit here. For once, I won't participate. I cross my legs and cross my arms and sit, all folded up like a pretzel. A pretzel in a wheelchair.

The room fills with good-humored chat and laughter as the others crank out flowers. I can hear relief in their voices; it's so strong I can almost smell it. I can definitely see it; Margie's face advertises it, plain as a billboard. The boom has been lowered and they're in trouble, but they don't care. They've decided the displeasure of a camp director is no big deal.

I'm frustrated. We were supposed to go horseback riding this morning and swimming this afternoon. I want to get some more photos. However, the punishment is due. What were we thinking?

The work becomes as rhythmical as a dance. They're singing. Camp songs, church songs, folk songs, rock 'n' roll, Motown. They take turns leading, all of them. Well, almost.

In her corner, Mary sits stiff on her cot, tapping an eyebrow.

In her corner, Dolly is sprawled in her chair, blabbing about her novella.

And in my spot, I smolder.

I resolve to sit out the day like a lump. I won't enjoy it. The program isn't about having fun. Engaged with their work, the others let me be. Just be.

By one o'clock, I am wondering about lunch. I'm not so much hungry as bored. The supplies are running out. All the crepe paper is gone, except for one yellow sheet, not enough to do anything with. The green tape ran out with the last coat hanger stem. Except for our own leis, the job—the supposedly all-day punishment—is done.

Carole sticks her head in the door and then calls outside, "You gotta see this, Sue. You want to come in here?"

They come in together. "Goodness gracious!" Sue is smiling in spite of herself. On every cot and footlocker, piled up in nutty profusion, are lurid bouquets, puffy pastel garlands. Margie's clean floor is dotted with confetti.

"Gather everything up," Sue says, "They've brought down the golf cart to take everything to the lodge."

Margie helps load the flowers. She comes back with boxed lunches stacked on her steady arms.

Sara says, "Sue, could you please ask the golf cart guy: What are they saying about us in the outside world? That we're exiled in Siberia?"

Margie guffaws. What does she know about Siberia?

Sue's face darkens above the flowers she is struggling to contain in her grasp.

The counselors go outside to the picnic table. I half want to join them and see if there's a breeze out there, but being trapped indoors is part of the punishment I've resolved to accept. It really is hot now. The humming fans serve only to mash the thick blanket of air against my body. My sweat has soaked through my clothes, and I'm stuck to my plastic seat.

Denise holds my sandwich to my mouth. I take a bite. It's cheese on Wonder Bread, but mainly what I taste is the smell of Denise's baby powder and perspiration. I think about Peggy Jo's asthma that doesn't bother her, because I feel like my chest is getting tight.

Peggy Jo tears Dolly's sandwich into bits and pushes them to the back of her mouth. Even with the lumps of bread in her throat, Dolly is trying to blab. The mess around her mouth makes my stomach reel.

"What about the apple?" Denise asks me.

I can't bite an apple. "No way." It's the first thing I've said for hours.

Margie starts to tidy up and goes for Mary's trash. On Mary's lap the food lies untouched. She probably doesn't know it's there. She's rocking on her cot and rubbing her earlobe.

"Mary, ain't you hungry?" Margie takes the sandwich out of the wax paper and gently touches it to Mary's lips.

The sandwich shoots across the room and rings against the screen opposite. Mary screams, like someone's beating her.

With two pops of the screen door, Sue and Carole are in the cabin. Mary is on the floor, rolled up in a tight, angry ball, banging her head against the linoleum.

"I ain't done nothing to her!"

Waving to Margie to be quiet, Sue and Carole walk slowly toward Mary. As they approach, Mary screams a strange unvaried scream and bangs her head with the same constant fury. They pause. They take one more small step, and Mary, as if provoked by the breach of some vital defense, kicks the iron bed frame so hard I think it too might fly across the room. She's up. Defending her territory. Lashing out. Carole hits the floor and rolls away. Sue steps back. I push the floor with my toe and back up too.

We give Mary all the room we can, and we wait. Still and silent, we wait, until the violence drains away and only a moan, a sad, slow moan, remains.

With firm, sure steps, Sue walks alone across the cabin and gently touches Mary's arm. This time Mary, as she's done so many times, stands up and follows Sue. They walk outside. Through the screens, we watch Sue walk Mary back and forth on the path. We hear the moan. The fury terrified me; this moan and the wordless agony it represents distress me even more.

Trembling, Margie sits on the edge of my bed and stud-ies her feet.

"Jean," she asks me, "is there something wrong with that girl's mind?"

Later, it will occur to me that this is a funny question. But right now I know she needs an answer. She needs to know it's not her fault. "Yes, some-thing's wrong with Ma-ry. De-fi-nite-ly. Her mind."

"I really did think so, you know."

Now that they have remembered to take her to the bath-room, Mary seems fine, but we're a little on edge. We've been inside all day, and now we're supposed to lie down and rest. Rest from what? No one wants to sleep, but soon they start dozing off. They sleep, but I don't. Neither does Sara.

Sara sits cross-legged on her cot and turns out Kleenex flowers. Ordinarily, my eye would follow that movement. However, I don't feel like watching those thin fingers pull tissues out of a box, those eyeteeth snap thread from a spool, that cot fill up with flowers.

Instead, I feel like smoldering. I've been smoldering, a dull lump of coal burning unnoticed, ever since Sara said such mean things and made everyone laugh. Now I won't let anyone poke at me. I won't flame up. I won't burn out.

I lie flat and look at the rafters. On the beam that runs over my cot, a spider has already rebuilt the web we knocked down this morning. I look for the spider, and I find it, suspended right over my feet. It seems to be waiting, just as still as I am. I lock my eyes on it. Which of us will be the first to move?

I think about what Sara said. A Norm in Crip's clothing. Until I came here, I never knew any Crips. I didn't think of myself as a Crip; I always figured that, beneath the surface, I am just like everyone else. A Norm at heart? Okay, maybe. But what's wrong with that? Why worry about it? Why care what Crips think?

Maybe because a Crip is what I am.

The idea almost makes me sick, so I seek another idea.

It's because I care for them. Not Crips as a group, but these particular Crips—Sara and Margie and the rest. It's my caring that gives them the power to hurt me.

They have the power. But no right to judge.

When rest period ends, cheerful talk starts up again. I stay on my cot. I'm hot and tired and my tailbone is sore from sitting motionless all morning on that plastic sling seat.

And, still, that spider hasn't moved.

Back in my chair, with Kleenex flowers pinned in my hair, I feel awfully silly. However, Margie's pleas wore down all my resistance. My yellow flowered tent-dress feels flimsy after so many days of stiff cotton shorts. But when I see everyone gather at the top of the hill, my spirits jerk up like a reflex. They all look so festive, so festive and silly, in their Kleenex leis. I decide to use up the rest of my film. Whether I like it or not, it is good to be outside again, out in the air, out with the group. It is good, too, to feel Willie standing behind me and leaning on my push handles.

"She's something else, isn't she?"

He's talking about Sara, and he makes me see it: She's being subversive.

"Yeah," I answer. "She's too much."

She isn't doing anything that could cause any complaint; she is just—being very amiable. She's been that way pretty much since the reverse telethon, but now she's taking it to a new height. Her mood is downright triumphant. As Peggy Jo threads her chair through the crowd, she greets people as though she's just back from a long and successful voyage.

"Hi, how are you? Good to see you! Looks like a great night for the ceremony!" She is a politician at the victory party, Miss America returning to her home airport, an astronaut splashing down. Victorious but humble; plain folks glad to be home.

"Your lei looks great with that shirt," she tells the quad. "Wait till you see all the wild decorations we made!" Her tone is inappropriate, no doubt; but who'd dare complain about excessive Camp Spirit? Willie is gently chuckling.

"Why can't she just leave well e-nough alone?" I ask him.

"I honestly don't know. Maybe she could, but she doesn't. Not ever. That's how she is. Nothing's ever 'well enough' with her. You just have to love it."

Peggy Jo pushes Sara up to us.

I feel Willie lean forward. Bowing maybe. "Welcome to Father Damian's leper colony."

"Go to hell, Willie."

"You ladies look lovely tonight. As always."

"Thanks. You look hideous. As always." He jostles my frame. I like feeling him laugh through my chrome, even though he is laughing at Sara's joke, and I know that all my irritation is evaporating in the low sun of late afternoon.

The doors open, and we're hit with the sweet smell of greasy food. I'm starving; that cheese sandwich wore off hours ago. I pass through the door and get my first sight of the decorations. Amazing! I can't suppress a squeal; my left arm shoots out with a little punch.

Sara catches my eye. "I'm really glad you like them!" is what she says. But she seems to say more: that she cares what I think. Even if I am a Norm in Crip's clothing, she cares what I think.

The centerpieces, a jumbled heap back in the cabin, now stand out against white tablecloths. Their colors are repeated in the red paper napkins, yellow plates, and multicolored streamers hanging from the rafters. The electric lights are dimmed beneath white Japanese lanterns. Most of the light comes from candles on the tables. For people who were cooped up all day, the effect is dramatic.

The room looks even better when filled with all the people in wild flowered clothes. I don't think it's much like Hawaii, but it is beautiful. And the strangeness of it—the wheelchairs, the crutches, the unusual bodies— all that makes it more beautiful, not less. It's exotic.

Hawaiian music comes over the PA. A floodlight comes on at the front of the lodge, and under the light two girl counselors dance the hula. Two grass-skirted sets of hips sway like palm trees in the breeze; two pairs of bare arms roll like waves on the beach. Each perfect body perfectly mirrors the other's graceful movements. As I watch, another image breaks into my head: I see two different sister bodies—those mismatched sisters—graceful Norm, gangly spazzo, the two I watched in the shower. Was it just two nights ago? For an instant, I see that girl again, I am that girl again, that spazzo girl with a grinning mouth and stomping heels. I can't bear it. I close my eyes. Another image pops up. A girl in a wheelchair, grinning like a fool and poking the linoleum with her heel, while a cute guy in cutoffs holds her hand and dances the shag the way it was meant to be done.

I draw my mind inside my body; so deep inside I can't see. I open my eyes, but instead of looking at the dancers, I watch Carole cut my meat. I open my mouth to the first bite, and my eyes dart to the dancers for just an instant. I fold my mouth around the salty ham, tear it with my teeth, mash it with my tongue, push it down my throat, and feel my stomach go to work on it. It is good. For the last couple of days, I've been nervous. I haven't been eating right. Carole gives me a forkful of rice and peas. Then pineapple, orange slices, and grapes. More ham.

My mouth is getting dry. Carole raises the straw to my lips. The cup of Hawaiian Punch has a little paper umbrella in it. It's so sweet I'm thirstier than ever. I'll get some water later.

They clear the dishes and bring out pineapple upside-down cake. The crumbly cake, tart pineapple, and sweet goo make me think of church suppers at home. It's amazing how much better I feel.

Mr. Bob stands. "It is my honor and privilege to present awards for the last session of 1970 at Camp Courage." At arts and crafts, we made picture frames of bamboo tied at the corners with twine. Now the frames are back, with certificates in them.

Sara whispers, "Get ready. This will take a while. There will be an award for absolutely everyone. Maybe even me."

She's right. Everyone gets a certificate for something, for Camp Spirit if nothing else.

The campers are recognized one by one, and I realize

that most of them are still strangers to me. I wonder about the things they could tell me. What's it like to spend half your childhood in the hospital? To be a Norm and then not be? And Butner. What's Butner really like? I am afraid even to ask myself, but at the same time I burn with wanting to know. I wonder about their families, where they live, how they live. In this place, so many little worlds come together, but most have failed to touch me. Maybe I've missed something important, and now it's too late even to find out what. I am wrapped in the soft sadness of an opportunity missed.

Mr. Bob is talking about Margie. "I personally have seen Margie, every meal, clearing the table, and wiping it till it shines. Congratulations, Margie." Flustered, joyous, Margie takes her certificate: Cleanest Camper.

As they go through the names of my cabinmates, I squirm. My name will be coming up. I hope I won't get Camp Spirit, but I can't think of anything I've achieved.

Then, it comes. Mr. Bob pats my head and dumps the certificate on my lap. "Best Bean Mosaic." I want to disappear. I didn't make the mosaic; Sara and Margie made it for me.

Margie jumps up. "Jean! We won!" She hugs me so hard it almost hurts, but she has shown me how to be proud of the award.

Next is Sara. "Member, Camper Council, 1970." I guess this is a historic fact, something Mr. Bob can't take away.

All he can do is declare, in black and white, that it's a council, not a Soviet. Graciously and entirely unlike someone in disgrace, Sara extends her hand to Mr. Bob, "Esteemed comandante, it was my pleasure to serve. Or at least try. Historical conditions were not quite ripe, but we may hope that the struggle—"

"That concludes the presentation of awards. I'd like to applaud all of you who achieved so much. Give yourselves a round of applause!"

Mr. Bob launches into a speech. "The awards represent a key ingredient in Camp Spirit—persistence. The best things don't come easy. You have to keep at it."

Willie creeps up behind us. "Sara, how many camp directors have you heard giving this speech?"

"Five, I think. In eight years."

"And how many times did they skip the awards for Cleanest Cabin and Best Cabin All Around?"

"Never before tonight."

"Congratulations! Our intelligence was that you had it nailed. That's why we didn't exert ourselves on Talent Night. We're saving it for next year. We'll grind you into dust."

"Have a good life, Willie."

"You too."

He fades into the shadows, and Mr. Bob's speech drones on. It's all about Camp Spirit, and Persistence, and Determination, and Courage. I wish he'd skip it. I've heard it before, too many times. At the telethons, they act like we show spirit in just being alive; persistence in not curling up and dying; determination in doing ordinary things; courage in showing our faces in public. It's insulting, really. I used to take it for granted, but no more. How can Mr. Bob still talk this way after the reverse telethon?

Didn't he get our point?

Singing, we make a slow procession to the lake. From now until morning, there is to be no talking.

We carry short candles in painted ice cream cups and go out into the night. The stars and moon are bright in a clear sky, but what I notice is the darkness; the outdoor lights are off. We make our way around the flagpole, down the hill, to the lake. "Kumbayah," we sing, "kumbayah."

The crickets and tree frogs sing loud enough to be heard over our singing, our strange singing that no longer sounds strange here. I speak the words. "Someone's singing, Lord, kumbayah. Someone's laughing, Lord, kumbayah. Someone's crying, Lord, kumbayah."

When we reach the edge of the lake, the singing stops, and Mr. Bob lights his candle. "We light our candles, passing the flame from hand to hand, as a symbol of all we have shared and all that we've learned. We put our candles on the lake as a symbol of our leaving this place. But we will take with us to our homes our own flame of Camp

Spirit." The counselors light their candles from Mr. Bob's and return to their campers and pass the flame on.

When the flame reaches Sara, the chain stops. "Margie," she whispers, breaking the silence, "this could be dangerous! Help us out."

Margie holds Sara's candle and lights mine from it. For a moment, our two wicks flare to join all three of us in golden light. Carefully, Margie lays my candle on my lap and sets Sara's in her hands. She lights her own candle from mine and passes it on to Denise. With the descent of silence—our first time coming together in silence—the chirps of crickets echo on the water. Tomorrow night I'll be in my own bed, listening through the open window to the crickets in my yard. It seems impossible.

Cabin by cabin, we go on the dock to see our candles lay on the water. From the dock, I look back at the shore at the candles resting in hands and on laps, hands and laps made anonymous, made uniform, by the darkness. I look down at the candles floating away, and at their light reflections shimmering on the black water.

As I watch the flickering lights drift away like tiny souls leaving, I think there is such a thing as Camp Spirit. But it isn't what Mr. Bob was talking about.

Mr. Bob may think he lit the first candle, but the flame is beyond anything he can control or even comprehend. Passing from hand to hand, the fire becomes new for each person. Camp Spirit is like that too—complex, changing, elusive. I think kindly of fire, its warmth and light, the fire of the hearth. A place where people gather for strength and nourishment. And I think of fire's power to consume and destroy. A raging force that blasts away the good and bad, the weak and strong, without discrimination, reducing them to their elements. And finally I open my heart to the small flame that flickers out in an instant, to endure only in a brief afterlife of memory. A spirit that exists only so long as it has something to act upon.

Margie takes my candle, and I see it settle on the water. As it drifts off, I deliberately look away. I don't want to follow its path. When I look at the water again, I can no longer distinguish my candle from the rest. I will never know what happens to it.

In silence, we roll up the hill. At the flagpole, invisible, without shadows, the boys go in one direction and the girls in the other to the places where we will sleep.

In silence, we get ready for bed. After nine nights, it has become a pattern that needs no words. Margie shakes out my dress and lays it across my footlocker. She puts the day's underwear, T-shirt, and socks in my laundry bag. Tomorrow or the next day, those things will be in my mother's washing machine, spinning around with the things they bring back from their vacation. Sand from the hills of Camp Courage will mix with sand brought from the ocean.

I sit on my bed and watch Sara get settled for the night. Carole pulls the curve out of her back, and her body-accordion expands. During my time here, I have ended most days watching her draw the night air deep into her lungs. She makes a tiny good-night salute as Carole stuffs two pillows under her bent knees. I'm not angry with her anymore. I want to tell her. In the morning I will.

The lights go out before taps sounds. In the dark, I hear whimpering. Carole comes out of the cubicle and sits on Margie's cot and strokes her forehead until I hear the sounds Margie makes in sleep. A short time later, there is a little sob, barely audible. Someone's crying, Lord. It sounds like Sara, but that can't be. I close my eyes and will myself not to join whoever it is. If I start crying, I'll go on for hours and keep everyone awake.

Day Ten

*Each ending is the beginning of a series of
events that are not being described.*

All morning I've wanted to tell Sara I'm not mad any-more, but there hasn't been time. We started with a wild rush of packing. At breakfast, the lodge was even noisier than usual; I couldn't possibly make myself heard over so many excited voices.

Now it's quiet. She and I are parked side by side at the picnic table in front of the lodge. She's reading the Sun-day paper, again commandeered from Mr. Bob; I have nothing to do but wait. I start to speak, but now I realize that no one—including Sara—has any idea how angry I've been. So how can I explain not being mad now? I want to say something, but what do I say?

She speaks first. "When are they coming for you?"

"Pret-ty soon, I think. Dad al-ways makes us get up real ear-ly. What a-bout you?"

"I'll have lunch here. I tell Grandmother to come late

because I like seeing all the families, the vehicles, the hellos, the good-byes. She'll come for me in a big blue Ford—an old-lady-mobile—and she'll bring some teenaged black girl to do the lifting. I'll stay with her till my mother gets back from Spain."

She goes back to her paper. We sit together in friendly silence, and I decide there's really no need to say anything. I watch the families arrive and try to guess who belongs to whom. It is interesting.

The bus from Butner has arrived, and the Butner people are being rounded up. The driver opens the back doors, and, with an aide, hoists Dolly, wheelchair and all, into the back compartment. The driver crawls around and gropes for belts to tie her up, and I think I see irritation move across his back. "Now I'll FINALLY have time for my NOVELLA," Dolly blabs, "Johnny CARSON . . . pretty risqué!" Aussie Robert tiptoes through the side door, dialing his phone. Mary follows him in and takes a seat, as tame today as yesterday she was wild: Mary, a little lamb. There are a half dozen others I've seen around. MRs. Aussies. Then last, I watch the aide park a wheelchair beside the front passenger seat.

At first I don't recognize the girl with very short hair. But when I see her grin at the driver, I know. It is the same face I saw a few nights ago, hair soaking wet, face bright under fluorescent light, grinning that grin at a perfect naked girl who was returning a bar of soap. Now that girl is headed home. Home to Butner. Desperately, I study her face, hoping to see something I didn't see before. I search for signs of mental retardation, autism, anything to make her different from me. But the only difference I see is the institutional haircut.

I watch her get good-bye hugs and speak to the driver, one careful syllable at a time. She takes his strong arm and steps up to the front seat and plops down. The driver closes the door. The aide collapses her chair and flings it in back with Dolly, then climbs in. The driver cranks the engine of the bus from Butner.

I would have gone to Butner, too, if my parents had listened to that doctor. Is that how it happens? I look through the bus windows at the people inside. How old were they when it happened? Will they be there when they're old? Will they die there? I watch the bus leave, and I want to scream.

But I don't scream. Screaming would do no good. Instead, I look at Sara. The bus from Butner doesn't seem to bother her. I guess she's seen it every year since she was a young child; maybe she's used to it. Or maybe Butner is one thing she can't talk about, can't explain, has no answer for. Maybe the whole crippled world lives with its fear of Butner, and places like Butner, by pretending not to notice.

Finally I manage to speak. "Hey, next year, write on your doc-tor's or-ders that you have to be in my ca-bin again." My voice sounds almost natural.

"Well, I would, but—I'm not coming back."

My body registers a jolt of surprise. "What?"

"I'm not coming back." She carefully folds the newspaper. "You got me thinking, when you asked why I keep coming if I don't like the activities. I gave you an answer, but it wasn't really true. There is no good reason.

"The truth is, when I came this time, I harbored a little impossible dream of my own. I—well, I thought I'd change things. I'd organize the campers and make this camp our own. I figured it wouldn't happen this year, but I could, sort of, plant the seed. But I realized it simply won't happen. Not ever. This is their place, not ours. Certainly not mine.

"So of course I came up with Plan B. If I couldn't fix it, I thought, well, I'll be like Samson—"

My surprise makes me snort.

"I know, it sounds ridiculous. I'm not exactly muscular, and you think of Samson as a muscleman. Victor Mature. But to me, Samson is a dear blind brother.

"You know, they gouge out his eyes and they hack off his hair and they make him a slave. They torture and tease him. That takes away his power, for a while. But he survives. By the time his hair grows back, his power is back too. But he doesn't tell a soul. And no one suspects, because he's still blind. And to them that means he's totally helpless. Pitiful. No threat.

"Well, blind Samson knows he can use that to get his revenge. The Philistines are all gathered in the temple, for this big festival they raise money for all year. Samson is part of the talent show. They come to gawk at him and congratulate themselves for being strong and powerful and doing such good works. A little boy leads Samson to the front of the temple, so all the gawkers can get a good view. Samson whines and shuffles, all weak and pitiful. He tells the little boy, 'I'm tired. I need something to lean on. How about the main support column for this whole structure? That would be good!' Well, the boy falls for it. Blind Samson leans and leans with all his famous strength. *Crash! Ka-boom!* He pulls the whole thing down! Down on the Philistines, the little boy, and Samson too."

I squeal. It's a horrible story, but I find myself a little thrilled.

She continues, ruefully. "So here I come, impossible dreaming of Samson, thinking I could put on a reverse telethon and, symbolically at least, pull it all down. But I didn't even make a crack. Yeah, sure, they didn't know what hit them—because they didn't get hit! Can you believe someone so brilliant could be such an idiot?"

I don't know what to say. I am beginning to try to absorb the simple fact that she isn't coming back.

"Well, my family's been making noises like I'm getting too old for camp. My grandmother wants to send Mama and me on a trip next year. London possibly. I'm going to start Norm school. Since I've been kicked out of Crip school, maybe it's time to exile myself from the Crip world altogether. I'll be a foreigner. You know, that's what you become when it gets impossible to live in the only place where you belong. You learn to sing the song of your people in a foreign land. Even if you're alone in Babylon and you have no one to sing it to but yourself."

I don't get it.

"Sorry," she says, "too much Bible all at once I guess. To you, I know Norm school is old hat. But it scares me to death. Last night, after lights out, I was actually crying! Something I've never done, not even when I was a little-kid first-time camper. It's just that I don't know how I'll get along in the Norm world. They'll never understand me, and I don't know if I even want to understand them. From what I've seen, they are a barbarous people.

"Jean, we don't have much time. You have to clue me in. Tell me what I need to know to survive in Norm school. What do they talk about?"

I'm happy to have a straightforward question. I think for just a moment. "I don't know what the boys talk a-bout. The girls talk a-bout boys."

She reacts with mock horror. "Boys? Is that all? Not politics? Not literature? Not philosophy? Not society? Not Marxism?"

I shake my head. When I calm a little, I say, "Well, at Cross-town High there is *one* lit-tle group of girls who don't talk a-bout boys."

"Hooray! There's hope! Tell me! Tell me! What?"

216

"They talk a-bout . . . hor-ses." At first she doesn't understand, but she thinks about it and then does a double take that climaxes with a groan.

"Did you say horses? Shit!"

We laugh heartily, but I'm uneasy. How will she get along? Norm kids won't sit still for her lectures or her weird Bible stories. She will indeed be a foreigner.

Around us cars are pulling in and pulling out with campers headed home. They stir the sand and gouge deep ruts in the ground. I feel sand on my arms and in my hair.

"Sa-ra, you should come back next year."

I want to say I've never had a friend like her. The girls and guys at school expect me to be something I'm not. At worst, I'm the mascot, an inferior who makes them look good. At best—the height of my aspirations up to now—not myself, but, merely, almost-one-of-them. I dress like them, but I look different. I go to the burger place with them, but I don't eat. I go to the ball games, but I try not to cheer too loud. People always comment on how I "fit right in." Before, I took that as a compliment, but now I know people only talk about how well you fit in if you don't, really.

I'll never be like Sara, but I don't have to be. With her, I can be myself. Even become myself. To become myself, I need this place, this strange place, whether I like it or not. And this place without Sara is inconceivable.

I want to say these things, but if I do, I might cry.

Sara looks at me. "I just can't come back. There's one

thing I haven't told you. When Bob—the Great White Father—had the little powwow with me yesterday, he told me I can't come back unless I actually sign a paper that I'll behave 'appropriately'."

"No way!"

"No way in hell. I'll never be what they think is appropriate. But, whether you like it or not, I admire you. Before I knew you, I thought you either resist or you are a no-good weasel. But *you* don't stay furious all the time, and you're no weasel. You're smart and you're for real. And you stay so calm. So cool. It blows me away."

"I only stay calm because I have to. If I get upset, I lose con-trol."

"Please, God, don't explain it away. When I go to Norm school, I'll try to take a vacation from impossible dreaming and remember that it's their school, not mine. I'll try to go with the flow, like you do, and get with the program. I'll try to be more like you."

She leans forward with laughter in her eyes. "Your shining example may sustain me in my journey into the Norm world. Don't mess it up for me, okay?"

I am fighting back tears. I can't speak.

Margie runs to us, scuffing up a little cloud of sand. "Hey, this is my ride. I'm gone. Y'all seen Willie?"

"No," Sara says. "He's probably hiding in the boys' room so he won't scare the parents. He'll know you would've said good-bye. Have a good trip home."

"Okay! See y'all next year."

Sara doesn't answer. Margie wraps her warm dusty arms around Sara and me and gives us happy kisses like a toddler going bye-bye. She grabs her suitcase and runs toward a white sedan. I realize I don't know what kind of home she's going to. A regular family, or some other place, maybe someplace where they taught her how to push wheelchairs and make beds with hospital corners? She's never spoken of home. I've never asked.

"Do something for me," Sara says as Margie's ride pulls out. "Come back next year and explain to Margie and Willie—and everyone—why I'm not back."

I stammer. How can I make Margie understand? How can I be the one to tell Willie, when Sara, who almost thinks he's beautiful, can't face him?

"And maybe, when two or three of you are gathered in my name, you'll do something maybe a little bit— inappropriate. Get some scheme going."

Around us, counselors ask questions, check luggage, count heads. Mr. Bob gives orders to the cleaning contractors. Bedding is coming up from the cabins, and plywood is going down, to board up for the winter. As the swarm of activity gets closer, my conversation with Sara comes to an end.

When my family arrives, it seems we've been apart for an age. They are brown from their week on the beach—

they've changed. Seeing them there, walking toward me, makes me realize how easily I fell into routines that didn't include them, how absent they have been from my mind. Did they forget me too?

"Hey, girl!" Dad yells. He kisses me with his scratchy face. "I see you're alive and kicking! None the worse for wear?" Mom leans on my push handles to plant a gentle kiss on my cheek. Cindy lifts my suitcase and groans like it weighs a ton. All at once they ask how am I doing, how was it, am I hungry, can I make it home without stopping. I am overwhelmed by the questions and by the sight of my family. I squeal.

"We're glad to see you too, honey," my mother says with a smile that has no worry behind it.

"Hello. Since Jean's apparently not doing proper introductions, permit me. My name is Sara. I was in Jean's cabin." She extends her thin hand to my dad like a grand Southern lady.

"Pleased to meet you, ma'am." I think he's half serious. "This is Jean's mama and her sister, Cindy."

"Did y'all have a good time at the beach?"

"Yes, thank you, we did." My mother looks flustered. Surprised.

Sara almost winks at me. "Looks like everybody got some sun!"

"Did we? Yes, ma'am, I reckon we did," my dad answers. Mom and Cindy exchange puzzled looks. Because they've

never known any Crips but me, they probably expect anyone in a wheelchair to stutter through all social situa-
tions. Little do they know.

From the side of her chair, Sara pulls out a sheet of
paper rolled up like a diploma. "Jean, this is the picture I
drew of the lake. I thought you might want it—I have six
or seven of them already. Cindy, can you take this? It's a
pastel drawing. Can you find a spot where it won't get
crushed or wet?"

Carole and Sue come to see me off and answer parental
questions. Denise, Peggy Jo, and Yvonne wave good-bye. I
can't say good-bye. I can't get my words together.

"Well, er, we'll be off," Dad says. "And it's so nice to
meet you, Miss Sara." He is almost bowing. "I hope our
Jean hasn't given you too hard a time! She can be a pesky
one!" He rubs my head until my hair sticks up. Sara is
highly amused.

Dad walks me into the front seat and loads my chair in
the back of the station wagon. Mom and Cindy take the
backseat.

"Safe journey," Sara says.

You too, I think, safe journey. But I still can't speak.

By the time the station wagon backs out, turns around,
and leaves the parking lot, I am sobbing uncontrollably.

"Jean, what's wrong?" Cindy asks.

Mom puts her arm around Cindy. "It's okay." She's

talking to Cindy, but I feel like she is talking to me too. In the rearview mirror, I see her stricken face. I know nothing could cause her more pain than to see me unhappy. She leans back and disappears from the mirror. Dad stares at the road.

Slowly we drive down the sandy road that laces through the pine woods and low hills to the exit of Camp Courage. From high overhead, sunlight comes through the windshield, intermittently blocked by limbs that reach across the road.

I can't stop crying. I am howling, howling like a baby, or not really like a baby, but like the grown-up spazzo-gone-amok that I am. The sobs have a will of their own, a will that won't submit to mine. I give up the battle and let go.

My thoughts race down the road faster than the station wagon can go. In my mind, I pass the camp sign and get on the paved road. From there it is a few miles to the highway and soon we will be in Crosstown. Back home.

Tonight, some relatives may show up for a cookout or potluck. By the time we sit down to eat, we'll fall back into old patterns. When Mom feeds me, she always combines the different foods on the fork. Dad feeds me the way he feeds himself. He eats all the meat, and then attacks the other dishes one by one. After supper we'll settle down and watch TV. It will be beautifully familiar. But now, part of the beauty will come from a sense that it is all so fragile.

In two weeks, I start my senior year. In a few months, I'll pose for my yearbook picture in a cap and gown, no doubt disheveled, my cap askew despite a dozen bobby pins, with a silly grin. After the diploma, I have no idea.

My old, automatic optimism is gone. Gone for good, I think. In its place I feel the seed of a different kind of hope, a heart that knows what rage is like and trust that lives with open eyes. Even in my turmoil, I can inventory my strengths. I am smart. I know how to work hard. I am loved. Most of all, I am loved. It is my family's love that saved me as a baby and has carried me safe thus far. Maybe someday it will fail me, but for now, just now, I will accept it as my best security. They are ready to give me everything I need, and they ask only that I be happy.

I'm not sure how, exactly, but I'm pretty sure I can do it. I think I can be happy, at least as happy as most people are. Butner will not have me. I have to believe that, although now I know that nothing is certain. One thing, however, I believe is almost certain: I'll never be "just like a normal girl." What I will be is beyond my imagining.

We reach the paved road, and I am still crying. My family ask no questions. I know they are mystified, but I can't worry about that, can't try to explain. I am going on a path of my own, a road they cannot take. I'll be alone, a separate person, even if, physically, I remain as close to them as ever. I'll take food from their hands, depend on them, live with them in love and harmony, but I will remain incomprehensible. Perhaps I will indulge them and let them think they understand, but they never will.

In the station wagon we sit so close we could easily hold hands, all four of us. But, waiting for my tears to be cried out, they leave me alone. As I feel them withdraw, I weep for the closeness we are losing. At the same time, I'm grateful to them for holding back, more grateful than I am for all the care they give me, more grateful than I am even for life itself. Now they are giving me a gift they don't really want to give. A gift they cannot even understand.

I have never felt more alone. I have never felt farther separated from my family. And in my whole life I have never loved them so much.

SARA J. BUCHANAN

ATTORNEY AT LAW

August 21, 2000

Dear Willie:

Since I did that TV talk show, I've heard from more friends and enemies and rank strangers than you could imagine—but all that's nothing compared to hearing from you!

First, thanks for the photo. I'm so happy to see that you've become even more hideous with the passage of the years. And a Dad-and-boy photo, no less! Your son is beautiful. Of course, I'm disappointed that you didn't sire a monster just like yourself, but no doubt you love him anyway.

Well, from the show, you know I'm considerably more decrepit but hanging on. Actually I'm astonished to find myself alive at middle age. Jerry Lewis always had me thinking I'd die as a sweet little child (which is odd, since I don't think I ever was a sweet little child), but now I have long gray hairs in my braid. I don't plan to dye them. It's good to know that time is passing.

I spend my time with lawyers and community organizers and academics and suchlike, and it's almost like the old Crip world—our own "old country"—never existed. I hold the world endurance record for telethon protesting, which you know about, but day in and day out I roam through the Norm world almost as if I belong in it. So much has changed! At least for me, and—now I know—for you too. I hope your computer genius has made you rich!

There was a girl at camp who wanted to be a pro-grammer like you. Do you remember a CP girl named Jean, who joined our little clique in my final year? She told me she wanted to go to Chapel Hill and study computers, and I squelched her most firmly. Back then, I was so sure of everything and thought it my duty to set everyone straight. Well, I hope she didn't listen to me (as I recall, she tended not to listen to me). I hope things worked out for her, but I don't know.

She wrote to me—three or four very concise typed letters. However, I didn't answer. I'd decided to "sever all ties" with cripplekind. Why? I don't know. At the time, I was struggling through *The Essential Lenin Reader* and seized on any opportunity I could find to be ruthless. Ah, youth!

I do wonder sometimes what became of them all. In fact, sometimes I lie awake at night and worry that Jean is languishing at Butner or some other desolate place, waiting for deliverance. In the wee hours, I resolve to use the law to liberate Jean or Margie or even Dolly. (I thought of her when Johnny Carson retired! Did you?)

But then morning comes, and I wake up to so many distractions and prior commitments—and maybe a little cowardice—and I say, no, deliverance is not my job. I say, if they need a deliverer, which probably they don't, a deliverer will come. Maybe some wild stuttering deliverer, like Moses, with a magic walking stick.

Yikes! What a lot of craziness I'm writing! It's just that it's been about three decades since I've been in communication with anyone who would have a CLUE about what I'm talking about. . . .

Back to your letter.

You have your nerve, asking about my love life, when you don't tell me who was brave enough to merge her DNA with yours and make a baby! Well, FYI, my love life is rich and varied. I love old city streets—there's nothing like bumping over slate sidewalks and brick streets in a rickety vintage E&J. I love soul food and my TV remote control. Stuff like that. I'm the same fussy old maid I was at age seventeen and rejoice that I'm finally aging into the part. I love "pure and chaste from afar," just

like the Sand Hills Community Youth Chorale always said
we should.

And I love you, dear hideous comrade of ancient
struggles. As I hope you've always known.

—Sara

ACKNOWLEDGMENTS

In the twelve years, off and on, that I have worked on this book, I have benefitted greatly from the comments of people who read it at various stages of its development and generously shared their unique perspectives, all different from mine: Barry Corbet, Phil Creel, Edda Erroll, Nancy Perry Graham, Brian Griffin, Laura Hershey, Cliff Honicker, Josephine Humphreys, Cass Irvin, Mary Johnson, Norma Mangum, Barbara Mattson, Lee Robinson, Larry Ruiz, Lee Smith, Vicky Wallace-Wuesthoff, and various family members—as well as a few agents and publishers who took the time to tell me why the answer was no. I'm delighted that ultimately the answer was yes from the Frances Goldin Literary Agency and Henry Holt and Company. My profound thanks go to them all. I also thank all of those who, way back in 1970 and before, had a vision of equality for people with disabilities and launched a human rights movement—entirely unknown to the people at Camp Courage—that continues to transform their lives, and ours.

ABOUT THE AUTHOR

Harriet McBryde Johnson went to schools for children with disabilities until age thirteen and to a cross-disability summer camp until age seventeen. She is still in contact with some of her friends from those times. Having continued her education in regular schools, she became a lawyer in 1985. Her solo practice in Charleston, South Carolina, emphasizes benefits and civil rights claims for poor and working people with disabilities. She has been active in the struggle for social justice, especially disability rights, and holds the world endurance record (fifteen years without interruption) for protesting the Jerry Lewis telethon for the Muscular Dystrophy Association. Ms. Johnson has written for the *New York Times Magazine* and is a frequent contributor to the disability press. She is also the author of a memoir, *Too Late to Die Young.*